PANTSULA BOY

and other African stories

Neil Thompson

Diadem Books

Diadem Books
Newcastle-upon-Tyne
www.diadembooks.org.uk

ISBN: 9798677509773

To our precious Penelope and Isla

'Unto the pure all things are pure.'

ACKNOWLEDGEMENTS

Thank you to my daughter Robyn and my wife Janet for all their help in the preparation of this anthology. My gratitude also goes to Sheena Carnie whose 'eagle eye' and encouragement shaped the final manuscript. And a sincere Thank You to Andrew Morrison for the sketch map in the story 'The Recce'.

Pantsula Boy and other African Stories is a work of fiction. The stories are, however, based on certain factual situations which I have either personally experienced or observed in others. Some events, places and dates have been altered in order to achieve continuity.

CONTENTS

GLOSSARY

Boeremusiek:	type of South African folk music, mainly instrumental
Dagga:	cannabis/marijuana
Ganja:	cannabis/marijuana
Kaross:	blanket made of animal skins
Klipspringer:	rock dwelling antelope (southern Africa)
Leguaan:	monitor lizard, also called iguana
Lord's Resistance Army:	rebel militia group (central Africa)
Mevrou:	Afrikaans title of address equivalent to Mrs
Milani:	Sir (respectful — Khoisan people)
Pantsula:	popular form of dance originating in the black townships of South Africa
Recce:	soldier in the specialist reconnaissance teams of the South African Special Forces 1966–1989
Rondawel:	traditional circular African dwelling
Setswana:	southern African language (of the Tswana people)
Skelm:	rogue
Sotho:	South African language (of the Sotho people)
Tokoloshe:	evil spirit (Zulu mythology)
ZAWA:	Zambian Wildlife Authority

THE LAST ARTIST

Namibia 1790

He was the last. That Nkwe knew for sure. There had been no reports of others like him. Not for a long time. Time that had slipped away with the full moon passing as often as the numbers in a vast herd of springbok.

As he lay there, his eyes adjusting to the early cerise dawn, a cool breeze blew through. It smelled so fragrant - of sage, and the floral scent of white-berry bushes.

'The bringer of rain,' Nkwe thought. 'The bringer of joy to these mountains. A good sign on this, my passing day.'

Today he would have the honour of joining his ancestors.

The previous night Nkwe had slept half upright, more often awake than asleep. He had not wanted his life spirit to leave him until he was ready; there were still a few final arrangements to be made.

The day had now come and Nkwe knew that he was well prepared. He looked forward to passing into the fire-mist of time.

Nkwe's father and his father before him, along with all their forefathers, were waiting. All the men who had painted in this isolated rugged wilderness would be there to greet him. As would the animals depicted on the walls around him — the ones they had respected and hunted. The animals that had sustained his family and all the others of his tribe through the years. The springbok and kudu, the oryx and gentle giraffe — they would be waiting there too.

Nkwe stood and stretched. His limbs were stiff from the manner in which he had rested. When the chill of the early morning burnt off, his body would feel looser and more relaxed. He drew the kaross more closely around his shoulders and walked slowly to the front of the cave.

Facing west he looked down and then across the Hungarob Ravine. The expanding glow of the dawn shimmered red on the huge boulders that sprawled along the opposite mountain ridge.

Out over the ravine a pair of black eagles was hunting. He watched as they lifted and glided, one soaring high, the other swooping low. Their hunting method and the grace and subtlety of their flight sent his mind and thoughts the same way. Dipping into the past. Rising into the future.

As they did every day and had done for so long, his reflections turned again to his family. The great moon had come and gone so many times.

What had become of them?

His woman who had been with him since childhood, with her timid nature and caring ways. Her warm, rounded body that pressed into his arc during the cold nights. And her sister, and her man the hunter. And all the children. What had become of them?

They had all gone down to the plains to forage and gather food. None had come back.

And when they did not return, his life, his inner purpose, slowly started dying down. Like a late evening's fire in the cave's stone circle.

But soon Nkwe would know. Perhaps they had survived but were now subjugated, slaves to the advancing tribes from the north. Or perhaps they had been killed by these new tall people. Or maybe chased and hounded into further isolation. Driven out into the deep desert where there was so little food and water.

Nkwe looked across at the hearth. His fire of the previous night was now only ash. The breeze grew a little stronger, lifting the fine cinders in a swirl across the face of his shelter.

Something within him lifted too.

He wondered whether he should eat. But there was no need. He had eaten the day before - roasted the remains of a rock rabbit and drunk a little of the honey-beer. The liquid's smoky sweetness was still discernible around his lips. It would be enough to nourish him on his journey.

Nkwe drew a deep breath; the time to prepare had come. He could no longer live alone. There was no point in living alone.

From the rear of his cave he fetched the log which he normally used as a bench when working. Taking his stone-axe, he neatly trimmed the log, shaping the sides so they were squarer. Then he carefully wedged it into a vertical fissure between two large boulders.

Satisfied that the log was firmly in place, he sat against it. The view down into the ravine and out across the plains was spectacular. It was a position that he had selected with care and precision.

Nkwe slid the kaross from around his shoulders and drew the rawhide tie-belt into his hands. Slowly he wrapped it around the log and then across his chest. He leaned forward, testing the knots. They held him securely.

Now he was ready.

With the sun warm on his bare chest and his eyes closed, his mind became still and started to sink. Hazy colours floated behind his eyelids.

At first the images appearing in front of him were faint. But slowly, as his breathing calmed, they became clearer. Skittish klipspringers leaping up high rock surfaces. Mountain zebra clattering along stony plateaux. A shy mongoose down in a watercourse.

From the ether, birds emerged. Desert wheatears that liked to flit about his cave dwelling. An augur buzzard perched on a rock outcrop. A streamlined peregrine, swift across the sky.

From the dune fields someone lifted a hand in greeting. It was his youngest son! The boy he had loved so much; the one he had trained to take over his craft. The son who had been killed by a marauding lion out in the river bed north of the mountains.

And there - his woman was there! Young, as she had been before they became husband and wife. She was dancing with other girls her age. They were doing the eland dance. She looked so young and pretty. Her apron was lifted and buttocks uncovered, undulating and provocative, ostrich-shell necklaces and bracelets softly clicking.

The wind gusted, carrying a sharp, light whistle through the rifts and crevices.

The last artist of the Brandberg sighed once. And was no more.

SIX WORDS

Rwanda 2012

He sat on the rickety wooden veranda that the old carpenter, Lazarus, had toiled over. Lazarus who cut joints that nearly fitted, and made dowels a little smaller than the holes they were destined to fill. Lazarus who used an ancient spirit level whose centre bubble almost certainly no longer levelled true. Lazarus who drove screws in with a hammer.

But down in the poverty-stricken village Lazarus was the only man who possessed any tools at all, meagre as they were. In the land of the blind, the one-eyed man is king.

James lifted his coffee cup and looked out over the wave-tumbling hills. The early morning mist was lifting slowly, and as the sun broke through, the purple and white wildflowers were opening, spreading out their colour and beauty.

The view took him in. As it always did. He could sit looking at it for hours on end. There would be birdsong, perhaps a hawk out scavenging, and occasionally a huge martial eagle would glide past on the hunt for live prey. In the far distance as the time of day changed so too would the colour of the Virunga Mountains. Grey, light blue, dark blue, green, bright green, blue then grey again.

But these days, especially during the last few weeks, he had been unsettled. There seemed to be a premonition hanging over him. His musings and inner reminiscences were increasingly interrupted. He thought he knew what it was...

They had been in Rwanda for eight years now.

Eight years in supposed retirement. Eight years voluntarily spent at the small clinic down in the village. Eight years nursing children who had no parents, then helping the same children become parents to their younger siblings. Eight years burying children too weak to pull through. Eight years of caring for victims of the genocide.

Mary was nearly seventy now, he seventy-three. He could see the spark in her eyes fading. The enthusiasm and bright hope in what they were doing was lessening each day. Even though she worked hard and gave of her love to him as she had always done, he knew that it was time to go home. They needed to be closer to their children and grandchildren.

James had made his decision; they would discuss it that night. At the end of this month they would give notice, work another three months, and then return to England. Hopefully the charity organisation they worked for would find some suitable replacements.

***

Slowly they drove down the winding track to the village, the sandy road washed out and rutted after recent heavy rains. James looked at Mary, and as he did so his wife reached across and rested her hand lightly on his knee. A small smile played across her lips; she could read him like a book.

In that moment a surge went through him - a surge of deep love and passion and desire. Mary was maturely beautiful, her face softly lined. He wanted to lean over and kiss her as he had when they were in their twenties. A tongue-deep kiss that would lead to more caressing and groping, clothes being opened. Then the moment passed and he smiled too.

In a small red-earth clearing the clinic stood neatly painted white, the corrugated iron roof a royal blue. To one side the distinctive Rwandan national flag fluttered gently in the light breeze.

For the first time in eight years the place was deserted.

Normally every morning there would be at least fifteen or twenty people waiting for treatment. Some of the people may have slept there overnight. Others would have walked in early from the surrounding areas. People up from the village or from the nearby school and child-mother centre.

Today there was no-one. Not a single person around.

'What's going on?' Mary asked, a furrow of worry creasing her forehead.

'I don't know,' James replied. 'You open up; I'll go to the village. Maybe someone important has died or somebody's called a community meeting that we weren't told about. I'll be back in twenty minutes.'

***

They encircled his vehicle just as he was turning around to drive back to the clinic. A shudder of fear jolted through him. An ice-hand clutched at his chest. His hands turned to stone on the steering wheel.

In that instant he knew why the vicinity was empty.

Everyone had fled up into the hills.

There were about ten of them - youths, mostly young boys barely into their teens. A rat pack. All were heavily armed with battered, poorly maintained AK47s, short barrelled machine guns he did not recognise, and bulky revolvers on low-slung waistbands. Some held heavy-bladed machetes almost as big as themselves.

It was their eyes and teeth, not their weapons, that scared him the most. Eyes red-veined and vacantly glazed; black rotten teeth exposed and spittled, lips pulled back in a grimace caused by disease and drugs and bush-liquor spirits.

One of them stepped forward. Through the fear a fleeting spark of recognition went through James' mind. The distinctive scar on the left cheek - a boy who had been a patient at their clinic some years ago. Why, he could not remember.

The scarred youth climbed into the passenger seat while all the others piled into the Land Rover's loading box.

'Who...who are you?' James stuttered, panic stricken.

'Hey, white man. Lord's Resistance Army, white man.' The AK47 was aimed directly at James' temple. 'Now drive. Go!'

All the way up to the clinic, as he jerked through the gears and struggled to hold the overloaded Land Rover on the bumpy track, James' mind grappled in trepidation.

His overriding concern was for Mary. A faint hope flickered; maybe she had understood the situation and run away too. Perhaps she'd realised why the patients and villagers alike had disappeared, were now all hiding in the surrounding uplands and low forest. Maybe somebody had stayed behind to warn her.

But no, there she was, standing in the doorway looking out. Waiting for him.

The rifle-barrel pressed even harder to his head. James stopped the vehicle and sat slumped, not daring to move. Not able to move. Had no strength to move.

In some crazed form of etiquette they didn't harm her in front of him.

They had an old filthy blanket which they drew around her. In a quick, smooth lift she was picked up, the blanket becoming a deep sagging hammock.

James saw her struggle and try to pull herself out, but the four boys holding the ends just shook the blanket vigorously and she slipped back down.

'Why?' he whispered hoarsely. 'Why this elderly woman, my wife, who has helped your people so much? Take me instead.'

'She may be old, but she is still pure.' The rebel leader cackled. 'My men believe she may be the one to cure them.'

'Cure them? Of what?' James' voice faltered; he knew that he was about to cry.

'Their bodies are diseased. Their minds are diseased. They will fuck her and then feed off her. She will be good for them. She is my gift to them,' the rebel asserted.

***

The man who lives in the care home near Oxford is just a shell. He has been there three years. To him time means nothing. One day is the same as three years.

His body is a breathing husk, his mind damaged and almost empty. His internal organs function in slow decay.

The short, sharp swinging blow he took to the head left him with only one thing. One slight yet terrible never-ending memory.

Six words.

Six words which he repeats over and over. Maybe sixty times an hour, more than six hundred times a day. Sometimes his lips form the words even while he is sedated and sleeps.

'She is my gift to them.'
'She is my gift to them.'
'She is my gift to them.'
'She is my gift to them.'

7

POLKA DANCING IN THE KALAHARI

Botswana 2012

The huge lion's gaze was impenetrable as I slowly backed off. The birds I had been watching were totally forgotten as the danger of the situation became clear.

I had been so engrossed in studying a steppe eagle through the spotting scope that the covert stealth of the lion's approach had caught me completely unaware.

The animal's golden eyes followed my movements as a light breeze ruffled the imposing black mane around its neck.

Trapped, I held my breath. Almost could not breathe. I backed up a little more. One step. Then another.

The surrounding bush seemed to have gone silent, inadvertent witness to the situation being played out. Even the small birds in the trees were quiet.

The lion sank into a low crouch. If it exploded towards me I knew there was little chance of escape or survival. Its powerful muscular limbs would propel it on to me in less than two bounds.

I reversed another step and felt the vehicle at my back. Inching sideways and reaching behind, I searched for the door handle.

The massive cat continued to watch me, eyes unblinking and fathomless.

Then, with an audible deep sigh, the lion lowered its head onto its paws. It was, almost immediately, fast asleep.

***

The faded sign at the turnoff to Middelputs read:

MOLOPO CAMP
- Restaurant
- Accommodation
- Camping
- Crafts
- Polka dancing
- Hiking

A look at my map indicated that to reach the camp I needed to take the next left turn, then first right and continue on for sixty-five kilometres.

I looked at the dashboard clock.

'Three thirty,' I said to myself. 'Better head that way otherwise I might struggle to find somewhere safe to stay tonight.'

For some reason, as I grew older, I tended to talk out loud to myself more often. It was probably as a result of still being on my own - unattached.

My friends would gently tease me about this. 'Watch out when you start replying to yourself,' or 'You need a girlfriend much younger than you; that will stop your talking,' or 'You really need a dog.'

However, in the here and now, the choice was simple - remain on the tarred road and have nowhere to stay, or cross into South Africa at Middelputs border post, drive down a rough, corrugated gravel road and sleep at the Molopo Camp.

The border officials were exuberantly friendly, even hasty. It was Friday afternoon after all; they just wanted to close up and go home. There was meat to be grilled on the open fire; there was beer and rum to be drunk.

I asked about the Molopo Camp. 'Yes,' they told me, 'the place is still open. The lady who owns it is there.'

In the end the road was not that bad. There were no other cars passing which helped to keep the dust down, so I left the windows open. The dry Kalahari air was fiercely hot. Even at four o'clock in the afternoon the reading on the car's external temperature gauge indicated 38°C.

The campsite was a little rundown; clearly not many people stayed there. But the ablutions were clean, and the elderly attendant smiling and helpful.

'Okay, *Milani*, I open the shower and make some hot water.'

I thanked him and turned away, but he clearly wanted to chat. He stood there, his soft khaki hat in his hands. 'My name is Alfred,' he said. 'You are on holiday, *Milani*?'

'Yes,' I replied. 'I'm travelling around. Mainly in Botswana.'

'That's good, *Milani*. There is much to see. You are from...where?'

'I now live in England, but I was born in South Africa.'

'Yes, I can still hear accent in your voice. And you are retired, *Milani*?'

'No, I still work.'

'Architect, doctor, *Milani*?'

'No, I'm an engineer. I work as a consultant - in the construction industry.'

'That's good, *Milani*, you are like me. Except my boss, she says that I am in the destruction industry - break everything I touch!' He laughed uproariously; there appeared to be only a few stumpy brown teeth left in his mouth.

'Tonight, *Milani*, you must come to the main camp,' he went on enthusiastically. 'Friday night here is party night.'

***

I stood at the bar watching the action, a glass of red wine and a carafe of water on the counter in front of me. The band was grouped in the far corner - drummer, accordionist, banjo player and two guitarists belting out a wide range of songs. They were a weather-beaten crew, clearly farmers and workers from the surrounding area.

Like many Afrikaners they were good musicians. Their variety of music was eclectic - country and western, driving rock from the seventies, blues from different eras. But when they turned to the traditional *boeremusiek* the dance floor really became packed, the partygoers waltzing and polka dancing to vigorous, unencumbered rhythms.

Young boys were swaying with their grandmothers, fathers were dancing with their daughters, single men cavorting and flirting with all of the women, whether encouraged to or not.

On the fringe of the action, dancing occasionally, but generally remaining self-possessed and aloof, a light-haired woman in a loose flowing skirt oversaw the bar. She made sure that the food and alcohol kept coming.

When the band stopped for a short break three other musicians stepped in. Fiddles wailing, they played hill-billy rock from the USA as authentic as the real thing.

I felt that it was time to turn in. I had swivelled to face the bar when a voice next to me spoke. 'Would you like to eat? I've brought you some meat. And salad. You look like a salad person.'

The light-haired woman stood there, a plate in either hand. An enquiring though slightly restrained smile played across her lips.

She was maturely attractive, with hair stylishly cut and tinted to make her look younger. Her eyes were remarkable, fine age-lines enhancing a brilliant cobalt blue. I wondered, fleetingly, where I had seen eyes like that before. As she spoke, her chin seemed to lift. At first the movement appeared to be slightly flirtatious, but I would later come to realise this was not the case. The action was more defensive than anything else.

'Thank you,' I replied. 'And why do you think I look like a salad person?'

'I don't know,' she grinned. 'Probably because you look so fit and healthy.'

'And probably because your attendant, Alfred, saw me go for a run just before the sun went down.'

'No, I saw you too. This lot here,' she gestured to the people surrounding us, 'this lot, and I mean the men, were already on their second or third beers by then. And there you are running in nearly forty degree heat.' She wagged her finger. 'You have to be a salad person.'

'There's no hope for me,' I said mock-seriously. 'I must be going crazy. Maybe it's the Kalahari sun that's affecting my mind.'

She laughed. 'That must be the reason. But then the Kalahari sun has probably made us all crazy too.' For a moment the lustre in her eyes appeared to fade. Despite the heat she seemed to shiver, and then whatever it was seemed to pass.

There was a brief silence between us.

Eventually she drew a breath. 'When are you leaving?'

'In the morning, but not too early. Probably around nine o'clock.'

'I'm so busy tonight. Will you...' she hesitated; her self-confidence seemed to have dissolved into shyness. 'Will you come for coffee...before...before you go?'

I nodded, surprised, and held out my hand. 'My name is Patrick. My friends call me Pat.'

'And I am Christine.' Her hand was calloused and strong.

***

'*Mevrou moet nou kom.* Please come now.' Alfred stood at the kitchen door.

'Alfred, I can't. I'm busy. Look at all this washing and ironing in front of me.'

'Please, *Mevrou.*' The man's voice sounded plaintive and scared. 'Please, *Mevrou.*'

Alfred's deeply creased, sunburnt face was quivering. She could not tell whether it was from dismay or fear. His cheeks were wet with what looked more like tears than perspiration. Stopping what she was doing, she studied him carefully.

'What is it, Alfred?' She could sense his alarm now. A tightness gripped her chest.

'Please, *Mevrou.*' The shock on his face was even more visibly intense in the sunlight.

With mounting concern, she tried to question him.

'By the river. The cave,' was all he would say. 'By the river. The cave,' he repeated.

Outside it was like a furnace, not a cloud in the sky. December in the Kalahari. But she had gone ice-cold.

The cave was the children's favourite play area. They had toys there. A little table and chairs. A sandpit. Samantha had dolls and teddy bears in tiny wooden beds; Michael had a track laid out for his toy cars.

'My God,' she blurted, as they got closer. 'What has happened? Has the roof fallen in?'

She started to run, feet slipping in her light sandals. 'Samantha, Michael!' she shouted. She was off-balance and uncontrolled, stumbling wildly.

Alfred grabbed her arm. '*Mevrou*, let us slow down.' He pulled hard and she swung around; stopped.

Her eyes were frantic. 'Alfred, we must get them out!'

'It is too late,' he said softly. 'It is too late.'

She tried to run again but he held her back. 'Come, more slowly. Whatever you see, I will try and help you.'

The cave was intact. As it had been for thousands of years. But the appalling scene that faced her would bring indelible change. It would damage her forever - emotional devastation and a mental emptiness that would take years to overcome.

One of Alfred's frayed old blankets covered the two small bodies. Gently, ever so carefully, he pulled back the blanket.

The children were lying on their sides.

'I closed their little eyes,' he whispered.

She dropped down and fell across the inert figures, tried to pull them closer. 'What happened?' she wailed.

'He...he murdered them,' Alfred uttered grimly.

The ground below the children's heads had turned black with blood. Clumps of hair and shards of bone and gristle had been blown into the sand.

'Who? How?' she cried. She scrabbled on the floor, trying to lift the children into her arms.

Alfred pulled her away. '*Mevrou*, he shot them. In the head. Left them here.'

'Alfred, let me go! These are my babies!'

Still he held on to her. 'No, *Mevrou*,' his voice thick. 'The damage is too much. We must get the police. We must go to the house and phone them.'

'Where is my husband?' she screamed, a raging fury engulfing her.

13

'He's over there,' he pointed. 'Under that tree.'

About two hundred metres away, she could see a figure slumped at the base of a large acacia.

'Is he..?' She could not finish the question.

Alfred nodded. '*Ja*, he murdered the children and then he killed himself.'

***

I could smell the coffee from some distance away. There are certain odours that I always savour, aromas that gave me special pleasure - expensive perfume like Chanel or Givenchy, the sweet scent of the Daphne bush in my garden at home, aromatic sage in the African veld, and freshly brewed coffee first thing in the morning.

Christine was sitting on the veranda. The table in front of her was set for a continental-style breakfast - cheese, sliced meats and tomatoes, preserves, fresh bread.

'Welcome,' she said. 'Please, sit down. Help yourself. I'm starving; when it's so busy like last night I don't get a chance to eat. Coffee?'

I watched as she poured. Her figure was shapely. She looked fit and trim, except I wondered - perhaps a little unfairly - whether she had undergone cosmetic surgery to her breasts. But then the thought passed.

Her hand shook slightly as she handed me the cup. 'I'm a little nervous,' she said. 'It's been a long time since I've done this.'

'Done what?' I asked.

'Had breakfast with a man on my own.'

'How long?'

'Nearly twenty-two years.' Her voice had a hard edge as she replied.

I looked at Christine closely and realised that she was indeed tense. She appeared to be dealing with some underlying stress and I couldn't understand it. Here was a good-looking woman who appeared to be self-sufficient and financially comfortable. Her home, from what I could see of it, was expensively furnished and spotlessly clean, with Delft crockery and Stuart crystal glassware displayed on the sideboard.

A minute later she gathered herself and gestured to the table. I could sense the tension lifting as we helped ourselves and began to eat.

I let her direct the conversation. I noticed it led away from herself and her circumstances. She seemed to be more interested in me.

Christine asked about my work and lifestyle, my interests and activities, and about my family ties, of which there were none. Now deceased, my parents were in their forties when they adopted me; I had just turned one. Without spoiling me, their love had been unconditional and special.

I had grown up without the urge or longing to find out who my birth parents were. I knew their names, but that had no significance or consequence to me.

I had never married; I think my independence made women edgy. A lover had once remarked caustically: 'You put us on pedestals. Sometimes we need to be treated as servants and sluts.' The relationship hadn't lasted long after that.

Then there were women, even wives of friends and associates, who seemed to want more of me than I was prepared to give. With dignity and sensitive respect, I turned them down; they still remained my friends.

'Christine, I think I should go now and leave you to your chores.' We had finished eating; our coffee cups stood empty.

She gazed at me as if weighing up what to say next. The blue in her eyes became darker, deeper, lustrous, almost violet. As had happened the previous evening, her eyes and the shape of her chin were again a reminder. Deep within my memory lay the image of someone - a similarly featured person. It was still very vague.

'Why don't you stay an extra day or two? There's quite a bit to see and do around here. You could take the access track to the west. It goes along the Molopo River to my neighbour's farm.' She pointed. 'He and his wife have a cheetah breeding programme there. And they rehabilitate raptors. You would be most welcome; they love talking about wildlife and are passionate about conservation.'

Another thought struck her. 'And at the end of my farm is a small Bushman community; Alfred can go with you to meet

15

them. They are fascinating people. I let them live as naturally as possible.' She touched a finger to her lips. 'Don't tell anyone, but I even let them hunt and forage in their traditional ways. Nobody else around here will allow that.'

***

In the end I did stay longer.

As Christine had indicated, the area was interesting and different. It drew me in, its vastness fascinating both in its grandeur and detail.

The grasses on the red dunes were still green and high, evidence of the recent good rains. The camelthorn trees in the riverbeds abounded with life — bees pollinating, flycatchers foraging down from perches onto the ground and then back up again, snakes in the social weaver birds' nests, the birds noisy and frenzied at their presence. Enthralled, I watched a Cape cobra as it glided along a branch and through a nest. A few minutes later it emerged with a tiny pale grey speckled egg.

In the evenings I spent time with Christine; we were enjoying each other's companionship. She would tell me of the neighbours - their difficulties, large and small, and stories of their everyday lives. She knew what the young people wanted. White children were eager to leave the working hardship of the farms, anxious about their futures, the lack of opportunities and jobs. The black and mixed-race children were equally desperate to have a better life than their parents. The older people worried about being left alone. Then there were the never-ending rumours of land appropriation. Almost overnight squatter settlements developed around them.

Christine remained an enigma. She was well-read and informed, but of herself she revealed nothing. Every so often there would be a glimpse of some unknown thing, a chink in her armour. I tried to draw her out, but just as I felt that she was about to tell me something personal her eyes appeared to glaze over and she changed the topic.

But there was one certain thing - deep in our roots, almost as if we might have known each other at some earlier time - an attraction was growing between us.

I knew it. She knew it.

On the fourth afternoon I went for a walk on my own. My mind needed clearing; my thoughts were scrambled. I wanted to sit quietly somewhere and decide what to do next.

The dusty path curved around Christine's home, then headed eastwards along a high bank above the Molopo River. In the distance, far down in the riverbed, I could see a few oryx meandering towards a water trough at the base of a windmill.

I wondered whether I should follow them, but then something glinting caught my eye. I looked carefully, eyes straining in the sharp sunlight. A little way below the ridge of the riverbank I could just make out Christine sitting in front of what appeared to be a steel cage.

I wanted to hang back and observe, but curiosity got the better of me and I made my way down to her. When I was still about twenty metres away I saw that she was not sitting at all. She was on her knees facing the iron bars - eyes closed, her shoulders shaking.

About to call out, I stopped, inhaled deeply, and silently squatted down. I tried to comprehend what was going on.

The iron bars formed a semi-circular protective grid in front of a sheltered cave. Fixed to the grid were two identical crosses. Below the crosses were ornate polished brass plaques inscribed with names and dates. Too far away for me to read, the writing was indistinct.

Christine was oblivious to my presence. After a while she slowly stood, still facing the mausoleum, her lips moving in silent speech. She sighed deeply, opened her eyes and saw me.

Alarmed, as if found guilty of some wrongdoing, she raised her hands to her mouth.

'May I come nearer?' I asked softly.

She nodded, her face etched with sorrow.

I wanted to put my arms around her, but hesitated and just took her hand instead. There was no resistance; if anything, she seemed to want my touch. She held my hand tightly as I read the inscriptions.

The memorial was twenty-two years old.

***

'So, Patrick, that is my story. That is why I am tied to this place - why I can never leave here. When my time comes, I want to be buried with my children.'

'Why did he do such a terrible thing?'

'He'd met another woman. Wanted a divorce.'

'And?'

'He said I could have the farm but he wanted custody of Michael and Samantha. He tried to make out that the farm was a bigger deal than my children.'

'Obviously you turned him down.'

'Over and over,' she nodded. 'Told him that at the end of the school term I was leaving, taking the children and going back to my parents who were prepared to help me.'

We were still holding hands; I drew her closer. 'What pushed him over the edge?'

I could see the question hurt her. She struggled to reply. 'I...I think there were two reasons. The first, and I only found that out later, was that his relationship with the other woman had broken down. She was pregnant, but not by him.' She shuddered. 'The second was that he saw me getting the children's clothes washed and ironed. Packing. Ready for leaving.'

'School holidays had started?' I asked.

'Almost; it was the last day of term.'

Before I spoke again, I put my arms around her, held her tightly, knowing what I next asked would be deeply painful. 'Did you not hear anything?'

'Oh, Patrick,' she wailed. 'He used a revolver, a large calibre, but with a silencer. Their injuries were so bad!'

I kept on holding her, knew that she had to keep on talking.

'It was my fault,' she whimpered. 'The packing. The leaving. Not trying to work things out. Not letting him touch me. Not understanding the male Afrikaner mentality - the shame he would have felt if we had left him. The damage to his name and his pride, his standing in the church and in the community. It was all my fault.'

'And you've carried this...this guilt with you all these years?'

'Yes. At the time I should have thought all those things through. Tried to forgive and forget, make our family life work again. Not even my mother knows much. I should have talked to her more, before and after, but I didn't.'

'And now?'

'You are the first person that knows everything. I have never confided in anyone else. There have been all sorts of rumours over the years.'

'And in your grief, you just ignored them?'

'Yes.'

'But how did you cope afterwards?' I asked. 'Emotionally, I mean.'

She pulled away slightly to face me. Her glorious eyes bore into mine. Tears were streaming down her face, mascara lines tracked and smeared.

'One morning, about a week later, I went outside. The funeral had taken place the day before.' She studied me carefully. 'I stood there watching the sunrise. My life had come to an end.'

Her hand tightened around mine as I waited for her to continue.

'From somewhere, out of nowhere, something came to me. A memory of what a boy had once said to me when I was about thirteen years old; he must have been a year older.' Her eyes never left my face. 'We had a subject at school called RE - Religious Education. The teacher was asking us about our churches and what we felt inside a church. The holiness of a church; a consecrated place - God's house. That sort of thing.'

Still I remained quiet.

'This boy, he said that he felt nothing. It was just a building. Without asking him for an explanation, the teacher expelled him from the class.'

Then I knew. I knew exactly who she was, but I said nothing.

'Later, at the lunch break, in the playground, I asked that boy what he meant. We were both so young, but he had wisdom beyond his years.'

The circle that life makes, I thought, amazed. *This is Chrissie Marais. Then so innocent and pretty, so timid, so trusting. And look at what fate has dealt her.*

My arm around her shoulders, I looked out across the dry landscape - the wide Molopo River below us, a river with no water, a river that never flowed, a river formed in sand and stone.

There were a few trees, clumps of tussocky grass. Arid, immense and stunningly beautiful.

I thought I knew what she was going to say next, but she surprised me.

'I once read the word *outlier*. Not knowing the meaning, I looked it up. It means, as far as I could understand it, a person who does not conform, one who thinks differently to those in the immediate society around them.'

Christine closed her eyes as she went on, concentrating, drawing from memory. 'Even at that age that boy was an outlier. He said...he said that our churches lay in the outdoors. Not confined in buildings. Buildings often, almost always, paid for by the very rich, or the very poor.'

Her voice trembled slightly. 'He said that the plains and mountains and valleys were our holy places. That if one listened carefully, one might hear the sound of voices when breezes blew or the wind gusted through the trees. If one looked up into the sky, the faces of loved ones would appear in the billowing of the clouds.'

Nearly forty years had passed since that day. I could still remember my words, still to this day believe the credence of them.

'That boy, that outlier, he believed that our spirits become free when we die. Free to circulate with their loved ones still living. He said that the Bushmen believe that the spirits of their forefathers and kin often reside in wild animals. He believed it too.'

She lifted my hand up in hers, held it high, pointing upwards. Her eyes, open again, now azure in colour, matching the vast skyscape. 'That is what I remembered. That is what came back to me that morning after the funeral.' Her tone was confident now. 'I remembered that the spirits of my darling girl and boy would always be with me, around me. I would see their faces in the clouds. Their voices would speak when the leaves rustled. The vocal arrow-marked babblers would bring their happy uncontrolled laughter to my ears.'

I wanted to interrupt; I had something that needed to be said. But I remained quiet. Just continued holding her. Twenty-two years of grief and pain were being purged; Christine needed the release.

'All these years I have lived here with my children buried in this cave. Just Alfred helping me. He has suffered too.' She pulled back her shoulders. 'I have struggled so much - psychologically, emotionally, physically. Years of drought. So alone. A single woman on a desert farm. But...' She gripped my hand tightly. 'But...I kept going, held myself together.'

Her eyes searched my own. They drew me in. 'Then four days ago,' she said, 'something wonderful happened to me. The Setswana have a saying for it. *Se se laotswêng.*'

'*Se se laotswêng?*'

'Yes. Do you know what it means?'

'I think so. Destiny?'

'Yes, but it's more than that. A closer explanation is probably a mixture of epiphany and revelation.'

For a moment neither of us spoke.

Her face looked different. Relaxed, softer, liberated.

'Chrissie,' I said softly. 'What are you really saying to me?'

She gazed at me, then smiled uninhibitedly. A smile that seemed new, untested. It enveloped me.

'Patrick, four days ago you arrived here. You know who I am, I saw it in your face just now.' She leaned forward and kissed me softly. 'Even after all these years I recognised you immediately when you arrived. You are that boy, Patrick, the one I loved as a little girl. The one I have always loved. You are that outlier.'

21

THE SACRED GARDEN

Guinea-Bissau 2013

They had him trussed up in some strange way. He tried to work it out.

He was naked, suspended six inches off the ground. His hands and legs were tied to the four corners of a vertical rectangular wooden frame. The frame, he remembered in his fear, was what the villagers used to hang and skin a calf. The only time he had ever seen it being used was when the chieftain had taken a new husband and a calf was slaughtered for the celebration feast.

The next day the leather hide had been coated in salt and stretched out on the frame to dry and cure.

His mind faltered, stampeding into horror. Was that what they planned for him?

And why was he tied like this? His hands were fastened with wrists facing forward. Grass-rope bonds circled his feet across the arches which were now bound backwards, ankles forcibly extended.

Another rope pulled his head sideways into a forty-five degree angle.

Initially all he had felt was discomfort, but now pain slowly kicked in as the blood-flow to his extremities diminished.

He thought that he had been hanging for about an hour when the chieftain appeared. Slowly and deliberately she tied one end of a length of thin woven twine to the tip of his penis, around the glans; the other end she attached to a timber wedge that had been driven into the ground below him.

Then she called out, a ululating piercing scream — the signal clear for all.

Slowly the villagers emerged from their huts. Others drifted in from the rice fields. The fishermen came up from the beach where they had been at their nets or working on their boats.

They all assembled in what appeared to be a pre-ordered manner.

On the left sat the smallest and youngest, babies remaining with their mothers. Then, increasing in size and strength, the line continued to the men and lastly, at the end of the horseshoe, stood the chieftain.

She moved forward, half a dozen club-like sticks in her hands. Walking down the line of people she handed them out. The lightest clubs for the little ones, and the heaviest she kept for herself.

***

'Philip, now that you have been ordained, have you decided what you want to do?' the bishop asked. 'When we last spoke you said that you might like to try missionary work.'

'Yes, Bishop,' Philip replied. 'I think that is what I would like to do. As you know, I have travelled recently so I have a better idea of where I'd like to go as well. With the church's help - and blessing, of course.'

'Yes, I heard you had been away. Where was it again? West Africa or somewhere like that?'

'Gambia and Senegal, Bishop.' In a flash the secrets shot through him. The tight Speedo he had worn on the beach, the encounters, jutting buttocks, black smooth oiled bodies so in contrast to his own. *Ganja* smoked and pills taken, driving the sex and exhilaration through the night.

His religious upbringing and training had disappeared into sensual hedonistic pleasure. Nobody to check on him. Nobody to reprimand him. Nobody to stop him.

Without any doubt it had been the best time of his life.

The bishop interrupted his reverie. 'Where would you like to go? I understand you speak other languages. French, Spanish?'

'No, I'm fluent in Portuguese. But my French is fair too.'

'Well, leave it with me; I'll see what can be done.'

Ten weeks passed before Philip heard anything more. Ten weeks of frustration. Boring work, elderly parishioners

23

complaining of colds and flu, cold wet climate, the few younger parishioners complaining, 'This weather makes me so depressed!'

The instruction eventually came. He hadn't expected a letter; he'd thought rather that he would be called in again.

ROMAN CATHOLIC DIOCESE OF LANCASTER

My dear Philip,

I have discussed your situation with my colleagues.

There was a little reluctance to assist you; apparently some rumours arose after your last holiday abroad. I will not go into any details here. But, in an effort to deal with those rumours and at the same time to help you, this is what we have decided to do:

We have had a request to assist the diocese in Guinea-Bissau. Apparently they are attempting to establish a mission on Ilha de Caravela, one of the Bijagos islands. This is to be in conjunction with a French NGO which has a clinic on the neighbouring island, the longer intention being to establish a clinic on Ilha de Caravela as well.

Bearing in mind that you speak both French and Portuguese (Bijagos was originally colonised by the Portuguese and some form of Portuguese Creole is spoken there), we felt that you should take up the position.

We have agreed on funding with the diocese in Bissau. They are expecting you at the end of the month. Your air ticket, travel expenses and other details will follow under separate cover. A small salary to cover your monthly costs has been arranged.

Please do a good job for the Lord and for our church.

With my own best wishes,
Go with God in your heart

Guinea-Bissau! Where was that? He'd been hoping that maybe Brazil or Mozambique would be suggested. Now he had been summarily told where the church wanted him to go.

He switched on his laptop and googled Guinea-Bissau. *Unstable government, Foreign Office warnings, tribal rivalries, high rainfall, strange religious practices, violence in the streets, shamanism, animalism.*

'They must be joking,' he said out loud. 'The bishop's missionary assignment has turned this into an exile.'

***

As he hung there - fixed and spread-eagled, his heart racing - his mind switched between outright terror and the memories of his time on the island. It was the beginning of his stay that he recalled first. Not the recent months when he had slipped into sloth and laziness, where one overriding thought dominated his day-to-day existence.

The early days had followed on so quickly. Twelve hours from England to West Africa. At three o'clock in the morning he arrived in Bissau. An elderly black man who spoke a little French was there to meet him.

'I take you to hotel. I fetch you at nine o'clock,' were the only words he spoke as Philip cleared customs and collected his luggage from the hand-pulled trailer.

The old man was there on time. They took a short drive through shabby Bissau down to the small, filth-strewn harbour. Philip tried to engage the man, but nothing was forthcoming. He merely pointed to a motorised fishing boat, where the grizzled skipper indicated that Philip should board. The rest was a blur.

Within minutes they were out in the open sea, crossing a deep channel with six-foot-high white-foamed grey waves bearing down on them. The noise of the sea and the 140-horsepower engine made conversation all but impossible.

Three hours later they landed at Ilha de Carache. The person receiving him was not from his church or from the French NGO, it was an elderly Italian nun, someone Philip judged to be in her late seventies. She was time-worn and frail, and walked with a stick, but her eyes were still bright and fervent.

25

'This is clinic,' she said, as she showed him around. 'Tomorrow you go Ilha de Caravela. To build like this. To also use for church, too.'

Philip's thoughts swirled. 'But I am no builder. What about materials? I don't think I can do this.'

She seemed unperturbed. 'You take paper. Draw this building. Take size. Take height. Look good now, so you remember.'

'But tools. And labour,' he spluttered. 'And, and ....'

'Some materials I will get for you. Iron for roof. And cement. I get from mainland.' She looked up at him. 'When you get to island, speak to chief. Explain. Fishermen will help you to make bricks. To cut wood for roof. To build.'

'And messages? Cell phone? How do I contact anyone?'

'Cell phone not work here. I will try and get radio contact for you. May take time to arrange. In meantime send message with fishermen.'

'But this is impossible!' Philip exclaimed.

'Remember who you are.' Now her voice was stern. 'You are like me. A missionary. Here to work. Here to give the people God's words. We are here to understand. You are here to understand.'

Then she was gone, hobbling up a path that led through the mangroves.

Philip never saw her or heard from her again. He would send messages, but only building materials ever came back.

***

The chieftain's command was softly uttered. They were not words Philip understood.

He felt a single soft blow just above the ankle.

Then came a second. And then a third - a little harder and slightly higher.

Out of the corner of his eye, Philip saw one child hand over a club to another.

The next blow caught him behind the right knee. There was a sharp, piercing pain as something tore behind the kneecap - probably ligaments or cartilage. His male appendage stretched in tension.

26

A girl of about eight delivered a wild swinging blow that caught the side of the same damaged knee. He cried out as the cartilage ripped further.

The grass twine cut into his penis.

A tough little boy who Philip knew suffered from glaucoma, had a slightly bigger club in his hands. He was studious in his approach. He lifted and swung viciously in one fluid motion. Philip screamed and then fainted.

The left patella was smashed; a bone splinter protruded through the tibial ligament.

***

The chieftain was in fact a woman. She received Philip in front of the doorway to her thatched hut. The surrounding area was spotlessly clean. A little garden planted to one side boasted tomatoes and native spinach, and what looked like cassava or okra, all neatly tended.

She had muscular arms and legs and stood tall, a formidable imposing figure. Her face was round, nose flat. Her eyes made Philip wince. They were huge and bulging with black orbs like coal-tar onyx.

She waited for Philip to speak.

He spoke hesitantly at first, as he drew the words and sentences from memory. He hadn't spoken Portuguese for a while and it sounded stilted, but she clearly understood what he was saying.

When he finished explaining, she spoke rapidly in Creole and then, with a dismissive gesture, turned and went back into her house.

The fisherman who had brought him over to Caravela said quietly, 'She says you can build. She says you can tell the people about your God. She says you cannot enter our sacred gardens.'

'That is all?'

'She says two men will be your helpers. On the days when they cannot fish.'

'But, as I understand it, that is on a Thursday only.'

'Yes. We are not allowed to fish on Thursdays. To protect the fish.'

Philip's head reeled. This could take years. The romantic zeal of being a missionary, originally deflated when he first found out about Guinea-Bissau, was completely flat now that he was here. The plans he had initially harboured included some language teaching in the mornings, or easy Bible class stories, then sleep and swim in the afternoons, with evenings spent in other ways. On Sundays a simple short sermon, then mixing and talking with those who were interested enough to attend.

But now he was being told, by both his church and this chieftain, to do everything himself. And that included erecting a simple building that could be used both as a church and a clinic. Find a way to get it all done.

His zeal was not that strong.

***

They threw water over him which brought him round. The terrible burning pain in his knees held him conscious.

The club had been changed to the next size up. A girl of fourteen had it gripped in hands and wrists toughened by years of pounding rice and grain. With a deadly accurate blow, she struck his lower back. Two of the lower vertebrae were immediately crushed. The following blow broke three more higher up. Then a clubbing overhand smashed his collar-bone, driving broken points of bone down into his shoulder blade.

He grunted back into unconsciousness, front teeth snapping through his tongue. An inch-long piece of it dropped out in a gush of blood-frothed spume.

The horseshoe crowd of villagers sat intent and deadly serious. All were silent. No-one moved.

***

Every Thursday the same two fishermen joined him. The older, a weather-beaten man in his fifties, clearly had some building knowledge. Vasco, the other, whom Philip judged to be between eighteen and twenty, was strong, smooth-skinned and good looking. He seldom spoke and clearly had some mental impairment, but always seemed gentle and docile.

They were hand-mixing concrete for the foundations when Vasco first removed his shirt. Perspiration burnished his skin,

28

droplets rolling down into the upper cleft between his buttocks. Black nipples shone in the bright sunlight.

Philip couldn't keep his eyes off him. A shiver of lust pierced his inner psyche. His scrotum tightened in desire.

***

The fifth largest club was now moving down the line of adults.

For some reason the men seemed to be more casual than the women - they took lazy loose swings. An ankle was cracked, and both of Philip's wrists were broken. But with the women it was different; they were savage and deliberate. Heavy blows pounded his sides, ribs and pelvic bones now ruptured or broken, held only in place by skin and shredded cartilage. The end of his penis lay in the dirt.

In the moments when Philip was lucid, when they threw water over him or jammed some snuff-like herb up his nostrils, he knew they were beating him to death. It was brutal and unrelenting.

From the moment they had seized him no-one had spoken to him. He hadn't been asked for an explanation. He hadn't been asked to plead. Not even after the first softer blows, when he could still speak.

But now he was beyond that. The pain was driving his mind into crimson madness. He could see strange inner lights, chimera-like shapes that floated spherically behind his eyeballs, split images of vague people. He had no idea what or who they were.

***

Philip took his time with Vasco.

Slight touches when they worked together. Jointly lifting a bag of cement, fingertips or hands in fleeting contact. Sitting slightly closer than normal at breaks for tea or lunch, a thigh or hip just glancing.

In the early evenings Philip secretly watched from afar, getting ever closer as Vasco bathed in the sea after a day's fishing. As Vasco soaped and splashed himself down, the priest's eyes would be fixed on the black man's well-built body clad in a pair of tight, faded blue shorts.

His breath caught in his throat the first time he saw Vasco remove his shorts and stand nude in the last sunlight. Philip's arousal was instantaneous and unrestrained. He jerked spontaneously into his hands.

His lust made him bolder. After a while Philip would walk down to the beach too each evening, soap and towel in hand. Quietly he would speak to Vasco without getting too near.

After a few occasions it seemed almost normal to Philip, their bathing together at the same time. Even Vasco in his slow, even-mannered way seemed to see nothing wrong. And no-one else appeared to be concerned.

Philip knew that it was only a question of time before he would be able to caress, to fondle the smooth-muscled body. The thought, and the anticipation, ordered his every day.

He had been on Ilha de Caravela just on four months. The small building's foundations were complete but nothing else had been done. He and the older fisherman spoke of making more bricks. They had yet to start.

Philip had abandoned any form of instruction, his religious training and will abandoned. The islanders knew he offered them nothing.

Sometimes his conscience would stir, but never for very long or with any intent.

He lived as the island men did - they fished and he built a little. In the early evenings the women would make food; they made for him too.

In the beginning he had worn his clerical collar with a T-shirt and cut-off jeans. Now he wore only the jeans.

Deeply tanned to a golden brown, all he wanted to do was cover Vasco's sculpted body with his own.

The first touches were exquisite. His fingers gliding up and down along Vasco's upper thighs, and closer, exploratory slow, to the firm bulge in the black man's shorts.

Vasco lay there in the sand, submissive and unconcerned.

Philip explored a little further, then on underneath Vasco's waistband, finger tips caressing the tight curls.

So completely had his desire overtaken him, that all sound was blocked out; his senses were fixed greedily on the ebony body next to him.

They came for him just as he began slipping Vasco's shorts down. With shouts of anger, almost hysterical rage, four men lifted him up. One aimed a punch; it buckled solidly into his solar plexus.

***

The chieftain looked at Philip square on, her face up close to his. There was a gruesome set to it, a demonic wrath that imprinted itself on the last tiny shred of sanity remaining within Philip's scorched mind.

With a short-swinging uppercut, her huge club crushed his bleeding testicles and the remainder of his penis. The men present instinctively winced, but Philip felt nothing; previous blows had already paralysed him from the waist down.

She lifted the club, her muscled forearms tense. A tight, crunching arc followed. The blow smashed through his face - the side that was angled up at forty-five degrees.

His head detached. The sight of her eyes shot with bloodlust and vengeance was the last terrible flash he took with him.

***

There are many strange, and not so strange, things in the Sacred Garden. Monkey pelts and putrid crocodile bodies hanging next to each other, tails intertwined. Rotting snakes nailed to overhanging boughs, even a hippo skin curiously painted blue and orange and white. Small bony heads of babies peek out from between exposed tree roots.

And tied upside down to a thick hanging vine is a crushed skull, a torn white piece of cloth fastened through the remaining eye socket. Sometimes when the sea-winds push through the surrounding forest, the cloth flutters like a spirit lost in the ether.

HELEN-JANINE

England 2014

It was the only message in my inbox.

'For the kind attention of Derek Hughes.'

At first I thought irritably it was just spam, but after a moment's deliberation I decided to open it.

The previous few nights I had slept badly, restless and unsettled, my sleep disturbed by recurring dreams of passages from my childhood. I would wake and then, as my mind calmed, doze again, sinking back to where the last dream had tailed off. As always, the face of the girl with her auburn hair was slightly different, almost blurred, but her body looked gracefully athletic. I knew who it was supposed to be - someone I hadn't seen, or heard of, in nearly forty years.

And now, as I read the email, the unease returned. The note was short and to the point:

Dear Mr Hughes

appreciate it if you would give me a call. My number is 0759 412 3440 (mobile).

I have a patient who needs your support urgently. I think you may be the only person who can help her.

Yours sincerely
Rosemary Clancy (MD)
Clinical Psychologist

What was going on here?

I sat back in my chair, trying to think which of my friends or acquaintances she might be referring to. I even broadened my contemplation to include female business associates.

There was no-one who came immediately to mind.

The initial anxiety I felt slowly dissipated, curiosity taking its place.

I picked up the telephone and then put it down; picked it up again. A few seconds later I was talking to Rosemary Clancy. She had answered the mobile number almost on the first ring.

'Mr Hughes, would it be possible for you to come and see me?' Her diction was modulated and clear, slightly tremulous; the voice of an older woman. *Probably older than me,* I thought.

'I have some time this week,' I replied. 'It depends on where you are, of course. And you will have to tell me what this is all about.'

'My rooms are in Oxford. I believe you live nearby?'

'Yes, I'm in Wallingford, about twenty-five minutes away.'

'Good. Could you possibly see me tomorrow morning? Will ten o'clock do?'

'I can, but Dr Clancy, you will have to give me some information.'

There was a pause before she spoke again. 'Mr Hughes, I will give you a name. If it spikes your interest, I am sure you will be here. If the name means nothing to you, then all I can do is thank you for calling so promptly.'

'I may need more than a name, Dr Clancy,' I replied, my tone a little sharp.

'Helen Ferguson.'

'I don't think I know a Helen Ferguson.'

'Her maiden name was Helen Wessels.'

I was so astonished, almost shocked, that I did not hear or respond to Dr Clancy saying goodbye. I sat back in a daze, looking out through the study window. My thoughts swirled, clouding through my psyche. *How was this possible?*

My dreams last night and the night before. The girl with the auburn hair - my first love. The first to share herself with me. All those years ago.

Helen Wessels.

When you looked into Rosemary Clancy's eyes you seemed to share what she had seen. Pain and despair, sunken minds and lost souls and, less often, happiness and upliftment. Her eyes were wide and ever-caring; they were always like that. She sat behind her desk, a frail-looking woman in her seventies. There were family photographs everywhere - they hung from all the walls, lined window sills and filled the occasional tables. Children on horseback and riding bicycles. Family parties and gatherings, barbeques and picnics. More formal photos of weddings and baptisms. Groups of people and individuals. There was even one of the current English Test cricket team.

She smiled as I took it all in. 'My grandson is standing third from left,' she said proudly. 'You may call me Rose or Auntie Rose; everyone does. And may I call you Derek?'

'Yes, of course.'

'You look tired, Derek.'

'I haven't slept well these last few nights.'

'Ah, I understand. Helen keeps me awake too,' she said enigmatically.

'I'm not too sure what's going on here,' I blurted out.

She nodded. 'I know. Let me get the tea and I'll start from the beginning.'

A few minutes later she was back. I helped her with the tray and we moved to a couch and an armchair near the window.

'I'll sit on the couch for a change.' She laughed and so did I, the tension within me lifting slightly.

'Derek, whatever I tell you is strictly confidential. Remember these are details of one of my patients.'

'And you are happy to share these with me?' I asked.

'Oh yes; I feel I have to. My patient needs help and we have to find a way.'

'Maybe before you start you could tell me how you found me.'

'It was luck really,' she replied. 'I was in my dentist's waiting room paging through a wildlife magazine when I saw an article written by a Derek Hughes.'

'And?'

'Remembering what Helen had once told me about you, in fact more than once, I wondered whether this was the same person.'

Rose sipped her tea and then went on. 'When I returned home, I did some research. It's not too difficult these days, is it?'

'I assume you found my website with my email address and contact details.'

'Yes.'

'So you put two and two together. Saw that I had grown up in Namibia - South West Africa in those days - and, of course, that Helen Wessels grew up there too.'

'Yes.'

'I presume Helen is your patient?'

Rose paused, considering her reply. 'Well, Derek, the answer to that is yes...and no.'

'That is a very strange answer, Doctor.'

She could see I was perplexed.

'I realise that. Let me tell you what I know. I may need to ask a question or two though, just to tie a few ends together.' Rose smiled gently, her eyes large and empathetic. 'Pour us some more tea and I'll start. And please, my dear, pass me the file on my desk. Sometimes I forget dates.'

I handed it over. The file was bulky, untidily filled with documents and reports.

She opened it and briefly scanned the inside of the cover, then closed the file and placed it on the couch next to her.

In her soft, almost brittle voice, this is what Rosemary Clancy told me:

'*In 1971 Helen Wessels completed her schooling in Windhoek, Namibia.*' The same year as I finished school. '*Some time in 1976 she moved to Cape Town in South Africa. There she met an Englishman, Terence Ferguson, and they married early in 1979. In 1982 a daughter was born. They remained in Cape Town until 1990. In April of the same year they moved to England. Early in 1991 the couple separated and were subsequently divorced. Helen and her daughter continued to live in England until Helen's tragic death in 2001.*'

I listened, almost unable to breathe, a spike of sadness piercing through me.

35

To anyone else the few facts looked so straightforward. But I knew they weren't, could never be.

'Is there more?' I whispered.

'Yes,' Rose replied. 'But I think you need to tell me what dismayed you.'

'It's the timeline,' I said.

'Yes, I thought it might be. The years match yours, don't they?'

'Yes. I finished my military service in 1975. In 1976 I moved to Cape Town. Spent five years doing a Master's degree in the Earth Sciences and then worked locally for another eight.'

'And then?'

'I moved to England in December 1989 and have been here ever since.'

For a moment the room was totally quiet. Rose sat still and said nothing. Her eyes did the enquiring.

I broke the silence. 'Don't tell me Helen moved to Oxford, too.'

'No, she lived in Henley-on-Thames. That is, after she and her husband separated.'

'My God, that's even closer to where I live.'

'Yes.'

My mind was like a crow's nest — jumbled thoughts and questions half interlocked, half loose and hazy. Inner alarm and worry were turning me cold; an involuntary shiver coursed through my body.

'It looks…' I hesitated, '…it looks like Helen followed me. Or stayed near me. For nearly twenty-five years.'

'Yes.' Rose Clancy's voice remained low, just penetrating my thoughts.

'She followed me, but never stalked me, never threatened me.'

'Yes, that is correct.'

'Why? Why did she never contact me? She obviously knew where I was. Why did she never answer any of the letters I wrote to her when I served in the army? What happened to her when I was serving?'

The doctor did not reply.

'Why?' I asked again.

36

Rose considered me carefully. 'Well, Derek, this is what we can do...' I detected a change in Rose's voice. Her tone was firmer and more controlled, as if she was preparing me for some mental impact.

'You can ask her,' Rose informed me.

'What? Whatever are you talking about?' My confusion turned to anger.

Rose was unperturbed. 'You shall just have to ask her yourself.'

'Dr Clancy, she died thirteen years ago. You told me so yourself, five minutes ago.' I stood abruptly and walked to the coat-stand where my jacket hung.

Falteringly Rose stood too and came over to me. 'Derek, please, I know this is all very sudden. And upsetting. But please will you give me a few more minutes to explain what I meant.'

Her eyes calmed me down. Taking my arm, she led me back to the armchair where I'd been sitting. For a while she didn't say anything. She seemed to be weighing up her thoughts.

'Derek, if you have time, I would like to take you somewhere. I think we have spoken enough. You will have to drive us there though. We can use my car. Normally my husband ferries me around, but he's away with one of our daughters today.'

I looked at her before replying, but she spoke again before I could.

'It will be easier for me to explain when we get there. And easier for you to understand.'

***

Driving through the green Oxfordshire countryside required me to concentrate. The unfamiliar car and narrow winding roads took my thoughts away from the last two hours spent in Rosemary Clancy's office.

When we reached the outskirts of the small village of Barford St Michael, Rose pointed ahead.

'There's a turnoff to the left. Can you see it? Where that small sign is? We need to turn there.'

A short private road ended at a pair of high timber gates. A tall upright man emerged from a security cubicle and came over to us.

'Good morning, Dr Clancy. I didn't know that you were visiting us today.' His hand touched his forehead in salute.

'No, Victor, I hadn't planned to, but I have a visitor that I'd like to show around.'

'That's no problem, Doctor; I'll let the duty manager know that you're on your way.' He studied me closely.

'Thank you, Victor.'

Slowly we motored into the estate, following a curved gravel driveway.

'What is this place?' I asked.

'This is the care home that my husband and I established thirty years ago. In those days we did everything ourselves; paid for everything ourselves. But now we are in partnership with others.'

I said nothing as we drove on, but questions were bubbling up inside me. After we parked, I helped her out of the car. Looking around I noticed everything was neat. The buildings were in good order, the gardens attractively laid out and well kept. In the near distance I could see two women on their knees, weeding or planting out a flower bed.

'Let's go inside, Derek, we have a small observation office where we can sit.'

Leaning on her walking stick, she slowly led me inside. A lady came forward to greet us, slightly officious but deferent to Rose; after a few words she seemed happy to leave us alone.

'Come this way, Derek, my dear.' I found my aggression and frustration ebbing; Rosemary Clancy was getting under my skin. She had the most disarming manner.

'What is this place exactly?'

We were looking through a large window into an adjacent room which, to me, appeared to be a working lounge.

There were, and I counted them, seven people busy at one sort of activity or another. In between their work stations were loose tables and chairs. Throw-rugs were scattered on the floor and, in one corner, there was a small open-plan kitchenette.

'My husband and I founded this home for patients who had become mentally scarred for one reason or another.' Rose looked across at me. 'Not for patients who are really damaged - not for the psychotics or schizophrenics. More for those who couldn't quite cope in the real world anymore.'

'Like a monastery or nunnery,' I suggested.

'Exactly,' Rose replied. 'But without any religious connotation or connections, without the dogma of any particular order. We wanted a place where patients could find peace and security. We offered an almost unconditional cloister.'

'So, there are some conditions?'

'A patient must do a meaningful duty or job whilst living here. They must have work; must try to earn their keep.'

'So, what do they do?'

'You saw the ladies working the garden?'

'Yes. Are they patients?'

'They are. As is Victor, the security guard.'

'What's wrong with him? He looks fine to me.'

'Victor served in the Iraq war. Got caught up in the Basra disaster and experienced the most terrible things. He suffers from post-traumatic stress disorder - PTSD as it's commonly known. Here at least he has found some peace.'

'The buildings look well maintained,' I commented.

'Yes, they're maintained and cleaned by our patients.'

A hiatus passed between us. The silence shifted as Rosemary Clancy eased herself into a chair.

'Why have you brought me here?' I blurted. 'And those strange statements of yours.'

'What statements, Derek?'

'Come on, Doctor, you've been toying with me. Maybe even manipulating me.'

'Really?'

'Of course. You said I'm the only one who can help a patient of yours. When I asked if Helen is your patient you said yes and no. What the heck does that mean?'

Rose just nodded her head.

'Then you said I must ask her the questions that I have. You said that twice.'

'Yes, that is correct.'

'Rose, you also told me that Helen has been dead for thirteen years!' My exasperation was growing.

'Derek, look into the room again,' she said, pointing. 'One of the women working there will answer your questions.'

I looked carefully. All the women appeared to be aged about forty. Helen, if she were alive, would be sixty-one, the same age as I was.

'Rose, you're doing it again.'

'Yes, I am,' she smiled. 'But no more. I am going to ask one of them to join us out in the garden. Wait for us there.'

***

'Hello, Derek, it's been a long time.' The voice came from behind me, subdued and slightly accented, the intonation distinctly South African.

I turned. The woman standing in front of me smiled demurely and then stepped forward. She reached out, gently caressing my cheek with the back of her right hand.

My breath was taken away. A lightning memory of a moment more than forty years before flashed through my mind. The last loving touch as I boarded the train that took me off to military service.

'I…I…don't know what to say,' I stammered.

'That's okay, Derek, I understand. I'm sure you are surprised to see me again.'

'Shall…shall we walk? Look at the gardens?' I suggested - anything to settle my uncertainty.

'Yes, that will be nice. Like we used to do back home in the old days.' She laughed softly. 'Let's go this way.'

She walked slightly ahead of me, and every so often when she stopped to speak the afternoon sunlight would catch her brown hair, enhancing streaks of deep red.

She looked a little overweight, but I couldn't be sure. The dress she wore was covered by a loose working smock, something she obviously wore to protect her normal clothes.

Her face was puffy as if from lack of sleep. Or perhaps she cried a lot. Now she looked happy, almost giddy. The questions tumbled out of her. I answered. The conversation seemed easier that way.

40

She asked after my parents and my sister. The two girls had been in the Girl Guides together. Asked whether I still worked and still played tennis.

'You know, Derek,' she said, grinning a little mischievously, 'I used to watch you playing football, especially when you were first picked to play for the national side. You were so graceful, turning left and right with such quick feet. I noticed that you could kick the ball equally well with either foot.'

And then she stopped and turned. Her dark eyes bore into me; they were flecked with gold. 'Derek, we are both much older now. Don't let the days go past anymore. Please come and see me whenever you can. I'm always here.'

And then, with a brief wave, she was gone.

A woman I had never seen before in my life.

***

I meandered back to the main building, my head awash with disbelief and half-forgotten remembrances.

Dr Clancy was waiting for me at the main door.

'Who is she?' I asked quietly. 'Who is she exactly?'

'The name on her birth certificate is Janine Ferguson.'

'Ferguson?'

'Yes, she is the daughter of Helen Wessels and Terence Ferguson.'

'But...'

'But you are puzzled. No, you are bewildered, are you not?'

'Yes.'

'I'll tell you why. Janine does not respond to her own name anymore.' Rose closely scrutinised my face as she said this. 'She responds only to the name Helen.'

'She is pretending to be her mother?' I asked incredulously.

'No, you don't understand. She is not pretending - she has become her mother.'

'What?'

'Janine has what we call Multiple Personality Disorder,' Rose went on. 'We know that there are at least three personalities within her. Her own, of course, which is now suppressed. That of her mother, which she has now assumed. We're not sure who the third one is, but we think it may be someone like a school

41

teacher or a female acquaintance of her mother's. We've never been able to find out.'

'But, Doctor, she knows things only her mother would have known. Intimate things. Personal things.'

'Yes. She has become her mother all of her waking hours. Why and how is beyond explanation.'

'They must have shared a lot,' I said.

As we walked slowly across to the car a further thought crossed my mind. 'In your email to me you said that your patient needed help urgently. And that I might be the only person able to help her. What did you mean by that?'

Rose eased herself into the passenger seat. 'We have intercoms and closed-circuit television in their bedrooms which we switch on at night. It is not something that we are very proud of, but it's considered a necessity.'

'I can understand that. They are patients after all.'

'Exactly.' Rose fastened her seatbelt as I started the car. 'In answer to your question, about a month ago we detected someone else in her room.'

'You saw someone on camera?'

'No, we only heard voices. That's what alarmed us.'

'In what way?'

'There was no-one else there.'

'Are you saying…' I left the sentence unfinished.

'Yes, my dear. A fourth personality is emerging. It may have always been there, but of that we cannot be sure.'

'And why is this of concern? Janine, or Helen as she is now, and I'm not sure if this is logical, seems rather open and pleasant. She seems well adjusted to her situation.'

Victor was waiting at the gates as we approached. Rose wound down her window and he came over to her. Again he saluted.

'Victor, this is Mr Derek Hughes. He may be visiting us from time to time in the near future.'

'Pleased to meet you, sir.' Carefully he scrutinised me again. 'You appear, sir, to have been a military man,' he stated authoritatively.

'I served in the South African Defence Force. Many years ago.'

'Which unit did you serve in, sir?'

'In reconnaissance.'

'You were a recce, sir? Fine units, sir. Fine, fine units. Small team missions; some of the best. Saw service in Angola then, sir?'

'Zambia and Mozambique too, but mainly Angola.'

'The South Africans were sold down the river there, sir. By us and by the Yanks. It was a damn shame, sir.'

With that he turned and opened the gates, saluting as we drove through.

'It's surprising that Victor knows of that obscure conflict,' I murmured to Rose.

'Other than being part of our security team, that's what he does. Reads and studies military history and conflict - all the time. His knowledge is profound.'

The traffic was heavier as we drove back into Oxford, the afternoon rush steadily building.

Neither of us spoke for a while.

I turned into Summertown.

'Derek, earlier you asked me why we were concerned.' Rose's voice broke my concentration.

'Yes, I did.'

'It's the fourth personality; it's affecting Janine.'

'In what way?' I asked.

'I won't go into the precise detail, but it's malevolent; it uses vulgar, sometimes even disturbed vile language.'

'And what effect does this have?'

'For all these years she's been on an even keel, but now she's sinking. She doesn't eat properly anymore. Her work is erratic. And her health and personal hygiene is declining.'

We stopped outside the doctor's house. I looked at her squarely.

'So you think I may be able to stabilise her again. Bring her back to what she was?'

'Yes, I do.'

***

All night I tossed and turned. Eventually, after hours of not being able to sleep, I went to my study. There I sat with a glass of

43

Laphroaig, hoping that the whisky's smoky peat taste would make me drowsy. If anything, it made me even more wide awake. The meeting with Janine, or Helen, resonated through my thoughts. I grappled to understand and comprehend the situation. The woman, Janine, was more than twenty years younger than I. But she was clearly also Helen, someone almost my own age.

I felt that Janine, with some due care to her appearance, would be appealing and attractive. But as Helen? We had been school sweethearts, young lovers, eyes only for each other in those late teen years. Where would that bring us now? How could I look at her, help her, with the old memories of those love-eager days surging up inside me?

It hardly seemed likely that I could stabilise Janine in some remote and detached way. And what did I know about treating mental illness? That field was far removed from my work in wildlife journalism and photography.

Round and round my thoughts went. I had lived alone for so many years, wrapped almost selfishly in the activities I wanted to do. Part of it was my own single-mindedness, and part of it was a cocoon to protect me from the loss of women I had loved. Helen Wessels all those years ago. And Francoise, the reckless French woman who, in 1993, tried to photograph a solitary irate old buffalo. She got too near and was trampled to death. I had helped dig her grave.

In the twenty-odd years since Francoise's death that protective shell around me had grown even thicker.

The early morning sounds penetrated through the open window as it slowly became lighter. Out in the trees the tawny owls were active, their calls clear and repetitive. The blackbirds and starlings flitted around the bird bath.

Was I prepared to try and intervene? Was there something in me beyond curiosity?

And then it became simple. I suppose most of us are the same - we all find it rewarding to fix something broken. I was no different.

Clinically, Dr Clancy said, Janine's personality had split. Janine was a different person; she lived as a different person to her physical being.

She had taken her mother's personality completely. Even the short time I had spent with her had convinced me of that.

I could walk away. But then what about the difficult unanswered questions? And the mystery and intrigue of it all?

But, most importantly, Dr Clancy had said that Janine was sinking. That my help would prove vital.

I knew then what I would do.

*****

I left it for that day. Just to mull over it all again. Then I rang Rosemary Clancy.

'Are you absolutely sure that Janine has this Multiple Personality Disorder?' I asked.

'As certain as we can be in these cases,' she replied. 'Various consultants and experts have examined her.'

'How long has she been like this?'

Rose paused before responding. 'Let's see...Helen died in June 2001.' I could hear papers rustling. 'Janine was referred to me in May the following year. By then she had become Helen almost totally. When the personality change started no-one really knows.'

'How did Helen die?' I asked quietly.

'She was out cycling with a friend. They were both knocked down and killed. Five o'clock on a Saturday afternoon in broad daylight. The man responsible had been in a pub most of the day.'

As she spoke my heartbeat seemed to stop, a reaction to the deep inner pain that bit into me.

'And...' I began as I gathered myself, 'what did Helen do...you know, for a living?'

'She was a dressmaker. And milliner. Apparently, she made the most beautiful clothes and hats.'

'And Janine - what can she do?'

'Derek, I think you now know the answer.'

'She's a dressmaker too?'

'Yes. That's how she earns her keep at our home. She specialises in wedding outfits.'

For a while it was quiet. As if one were waiting for the other to speak.

'Derek, are you still there?'

'Yes, I'm here. I'll help Janine if I can. What do you think I should do?'

***

Every Wednesday I went to visit her.

The first few times it felt as if I were visiting a patient in hospital. I wanted to do the right thing, but also wanted to leave as soon as was politely possible.

Later the visits to Janine, or Helen-Janine as I named her to myself, became different. At first I could not fully comprehend why.

I now looked forward to the Wednesdays and always made sure to keep the day completely free. On the fifth visit I took her a bouquet of flowers - lilac roses that traced a subtle perfume in my car.

After that I always took her something small. Each time the wondrous look on her face was a reward and a reminder to me. Over forty years ago her mother used to react in exactly the same way.

It was this look, and more, that made the Wednesdays enjoyable.

Helen-Janine was changing. Not in personality, more in her appearance and health. The puffiness had gone from her face and her skin had cleared. She looked vibrant and refreshed.

Weather permitting, she exercised outdoors most days. Her figure had become firmer and fitter, her arms and shoulders tanned a light golden brown.

Realisation and understanding came to me slowly. The initial resistance from deep within my inner self was breaking down, my natural caution slowly dissolving.

I was becoming deeply attracted to a woman many years younger than I. And yet she was also a woman I had known and who had followed me all my life.

I knew the emotional ground was treacherous. I knew that Helen-Janine was unstable. I knew that ethics and decency could be questioned.

But at that point in time we were a man and woman finding each other.

The circumstances no longer appeared so important.

***

Rosemary Clancy rang on three occasions. She, too, confirmed the overall improvement in Helen-Janine. Her views and impressions matched my own.

At the end of the third call the warning came. 'Derek, there is a report, or should I say an observation, that during your visit last week you and Janine were seen holding hands. Maybe a little more.'

I saw no point in trying to deny it.

'I must warn you, please Derek, please be circumspect.'

'Why do you say that?'

'As I told you before, she voluntarily came to stay with us as a patient.'

'Yes,' I acknowledged.

Rose took a deep breath. 'If I felt there was danger, either to her health or to your well-being...' She stopped.

I sensed she was trying to find the right words. 'What are you trying to say?' I asked.

'If I felt that the risk was too great, I could have her sectioned.'

'Sectioned?'

'Committed to a psychiatric hospital.'

'You mean locked away?' I exclaimed.

'Not totally, but she would be placed under greater restriction.'

'Would you do that?'

'Only if, as I said, the risks outweighed everything else.'

'But you must agree that her health - both physical and mental - is much better.'

'Yes, Derek, that is why I am only asking you to be careful. Be prudent.'

'At the moment she is so well,' I said. 'Dr Clancy?'

'Yes, my dear.'

I wanted to tell her how I felt about Helen-Janine. How that, after all these years, I felt eager to be with a woman again. Hungry to share things again. My life had, for too long, been lonely and austere. But I couldn't find the words to articulate my thoughts.

'Dr Clancy, you may be right. Your words are wise and I'll consider very carefully what you have said. Thank you for the call.'

I felt, and sounded, slightly angry and pompous.

***

I had spent the last three days at a conference in Madrid before catching an early morning flight back home. Now, standing in the kitchen waiting for the kettle to boil, I pondered whether to open the post first or to listen to the voicemails. I picked up the phone. There seemed to be more messages than normal. The first one was from Rosemary Clancy asking me to call her as soon as possible. The message had been left over forty-eight hours ago. She sounded a little anxious. I decided I would make a cup of tea and then ring her. Another few minutes wouldn't make much difference.

The doorbell rang softly. Once, and then again.

She was standing there smiling as I opened the door, her hand lifted, about to press the bell again.

'My God, Helen, what are you doing here?'

'I've come to see you for a change.' The back of her hand ran softly down the side of my face.

'This is a surprise! How did you get here?'

'We were on a group outing to Oxford. I slipped away and caught the bus over to you.' An impish grin played on her lips. 'Can I come in?'

'Of course, of course. I've just got back from Spain.'

'Yes, you said you were going. I've always wanted to go there.'

Helen-Janine came inside and I helped her out of the light jacket around her shoulders. Her hair shone clean and lustrous, scented an elusive fragrance of lime or lemon.

She curved into me, her back tight to my chest.

'Helen?'

She reached up and placed a finger over my lips.

'Derek, I have waited nearly a lifetime to be with you. To be alone again with you. Show me your home. And,' lifting and turning her lips into my neck, 'show me your bedroom.'

***

The morning had stretched into the afternoon, languorous and drawn out as we made love. The curtains were open to let the sunlight in; the rays over her body were bold and erotic. She was full around the hips and breasts, her legs and arms strong and firm. There, with her head on my chest, I compared her flawless skin against my own. The contrast in our ages was clearly evident. It seemed to be of no concern to her.

Lazily I caressed her buttocks. Helen-Janine moved slowly with my hand, sighing softly in pleasure.

And as we lay there, awake and resting, I asked her the questions that Dr Clancy had not been able to answer. Ones that I had not yet had the courage to approach.

'How did you always know where I was? And why follow me from town to town, and then from South Africa to England?'

'It was so easy, my darling. Do you remember my brother Frank?'

'Yes.' Frank had been two years older than I; a policeman from the day he left school.

'Well, he left the police force after a few years and went private.'

'Went private?'

'Yes,' she continued, 'he became a private detective. For many years he had the largest agency in Cape Town. He employed many disgruntled ex-policemen.'

'So he kept tabs on me.' My voice sounded sharp.

'Yes, my darling. But in a good way. Just so that I knew you were well.' Her hand squeezed me soothingly.

'Why didn't you contact me?'

'I was hurt, but healing. It seemed to be for the best. For you and for me.'

Helen-Janine shifted further down on me. My arousal grew as I felt her breath across my belly.

'And my letters? I wrote to you so many times.'

Her body stiffened as if in surprise. She whispered something that I couldn't hear, the sound concealed within herself. Drawing her fingers to her mouth and moistening them, she reached down and fondled me more steadily, her touch at first gently tender and then ferociously eager.

I was lost in sensation and lust.

***

I sat on the edge of the bed, naked and replete. The sun was going down, and through the open window the sky was fading into muted orange.

Helen-Janine was in the shower, the water turned full and loud. Then the bed sagged slightly and I felt her behind me. Her slick breasts pressed into my back, left arm wrapped around me.

Eyes half-closed in the intimacy of her embrace, two thoughts flitted through my mind. *I don't think she knows about my letters. I wonder why. And why is the shower still running?*

The glint came from over my right shoulder. I opened my eyes wide. In an ephemeral flash I saw a thick, needle-sharp pin about four inches long.

Her hand plunged forward. There was a searing, grinding pain just to the left of my Adam's apple.

I jerked forward to try and free myself. The pin penetrated even deeper. Both her arms were tightly clamped around me. I tore at them, trying to free myself.

And then it came. It seemed to be so quick. The fading of strength. The fading of sight.

I looked down. My lower body appeared disconnected. My carotid pumped. Blood spewed everywhere as my heart pounded in fear and desperation.

I was drifting. Fainting. My vision lost in a shadowing blackness.

I heard a shuddered agonised gasp, 'Aargh ...aargh.'

South Africa 2020

She lives out on the edge of the Langebaan Lagoon. A seamstress who makes wedding dresses for Cape Town's wealthy and elite.

Her daughter is nearly six. A little tomboy who is always outdoors playing in the garden or on the beach. Sometimes she helps the fishermen clean their catch or mend their nets. They don't mind; the girl has no father so they all look after her.

In her early pregnancy the woman had considered having an abortion, but after careful reflection decided against it. Her

50

daughter's father had been good for her. And to her. Her daughter would surely bear those characteristics too.

Derek had freed her from the demons. Freed her from the memory of her possessive and overpowering mother. Freed her from the memory of her abusive and vile father, a father who had broken her hymen with his finger on her tenth birthday.

And now, when the past comes to haunt - the lost years spent in the Clancy's care home, the fiends that had almost possessed her, the letters she should have known about, the gushed fountains of blood on the bed sheets - she knows how to cope.

She has a tin of cigarette papers and some coarse weed that the old Malay gardener sells her.

Her focus is deliberate. She rolls the joint and lights up.

A deep inhale. The sweet-hemp smoke filters through her facial passages.

Her mind slowly settles back into equilibrium and peace.

PANTSULA BOY

South Africa 2018

His lucky day had arrived. Of that he was sure.

He looked into the cracked mirror and grinned. His split visage reflected back a demonic sneer.

Even the fetid faeces stench from the close-to-overflowing long drop failed to irritate him as it usually did. The toilet had been in his granny's backyard for more than fifty years. As far as he knew there had never been an attempt to improve the situation, nor even a discussion on how to improve it.

'Man, I feel great today,' Hotstick said to the fractured likeness facing him.

His name was one that he had assumed; a badge of honour. A name he had given himself when, at the age of twelve, he impregnated his cousin of thirteen. A tiny baby arrived precisely thirty-two weeks and four days later.

Cleophas 'Hotstick' Rabusana's spirits were high. What did that stupid radio say? *He felt epic.*

His hotstick felt really good too. 'Well exercised,' he laughed to his reflection.

Last night had done that. The happy-go-lucky girl from three shacks down the road loving him hard for a few hours. Some cash made her agreeably compliant. Vaseline had made the going smoother. An ecstasy pill had made it vigorously adventurous.

And now today he was starting his first job. His first contract.

He was now a contractor - a businessman at seventeen years old! Work for his team!

The gang, his team, all younger than him, would arrive soon. After a short meeting they would head off together. Bighead Ramphele who loved watching football and doing nothing else. Bible quoting Preacher Buthelezi who lived only for stealing.

52

And Eunice Sweethand Ndhlovu, a slender but tough girl who fisted out hand jobs for one hundred bucks a throw. A razor-sharp knife remained concealed in her left hand should a client become too touchy or frisky.

***

Their first job was a cleaning contract.

The Malawian trafficker Bigman Banda lived in a large fancy house on the outskirts of Tembisa. Apparently it desperately needed cleaning. Hotstick had heard that it was like a pigsty inside. But that was fine. Good money had been agreed on and they were to clean it twice a week.

Why the Malawian had selected them for the work was something Hotstick hadn't quite puzzled out yet. Maybe they were being tested. Maybe Bigman Banda wanted them for something more illegal and lucrative in the future but first wanted to make sure they could be trusted.

Hotstick's instructions to his team were clear: 'If we recover anything of value in the mess we leave it carefully for Bigman to find. We are there to earn money, not to steal!'

Preacher shook his head in mock wonder and smirked inanely.

***

Hotstick had further plans for the evening after they were finished. With money in his pocket he felt sure that he could persuade Dorothy to go out with him. She liked cash and clothes and perfumes and hairdos. The last three varied in order of preference, all dependent on the financial circumstances of her suitors.

Dorothy possessed the looks and the body. And a cunning eye for a man on the up.

'I just want to climb all over her,' Hotstick told his crew.

'Hey, my brother, you are playing with fire from hell,' Preacher said. 'She will turn you into a pillar of salt.'

The others laughed.

'She has other boyfriends,' Preacher went on. 'And you know her father; he rules his bar with a bullwhip. He's a cruel bastard that one.'

Hotstick pretended to have gone deaf.

***

The work had gone well. It had just taken longer than expected. The Malawian's house was filthier than reported.

There were all manner of items among the debris and rubbish. KFC and MacDonald's food packets and cartons were strewn everywhere. The counters were layered in coats of putrescent grease. Numerous stains that looked like excrement marked the carpets.

They found two ladies' watches, a cell phone, condoms - used and unused - as well as strangely shaped and ridiculously proportioned sex toys. Bighead offered a large pink dildo to Eunice who succinctly told him to try it himself and to fuck off.

There were also half drunk bottles of liquor and dubious pills of various colours and descriptions. Behind one of the sofas Preacher found a prosthetic hand.

Slowly and thoroughly, Hotstick and his team cleaned the place. All the retrieved items were laid out neatly on the dining room table.

As they were finishing up there was a brief delay while they waited for Preacher to use up some spare cash burning a hole in his pocket. In one of the bathrooms Eunice quickly and efficiently relieved him of both his money and his semen.

But then the work was done and the four of them were out of there.

***

Friday night and the One Place Drinking Bar was heaving. It was so crowded that the revellers had moved out onto the street.

They danced and drank and shouted. Hard drugs, soft drugs and 'recreational' drugs changed hands. Marijuana smoke hazed and swirled. Pantsula music thumped at full blast. The spivs and the gangsters mingled among the good-time girls and prostitutes.

The only authority was the bar owner - and his henchmen.

Under a streetlight Hotstick danced with Dorothy. Her blue-sequinned top shimmered and gyrated; he had his hands low on her waist, fingers exploring her tight satin-clad buttocks. The pills in his pocket were for later.

Hotstick was where he wanted to be.

The *crack* almost took his head off. Hotstick threw his hands up to his throat, choking and stumbling back. The end of the leather whip was coiled around his neck. He felt another vicious tug backwards.

Then Hotstick felt the knife. The blistering pain carved through flesh and bone as it went through him. His eyes clouding, he looked down and saw the point emerging just above his midriff.

He staggered and slowly fell; a paroxysm of darkness jolted him into death.

His lucky day had ended as surely as it had begun.

AMIRA

South Africa 2018

'Good morning, Wendy's Guesthouse!' She answered the phone and listened closely. 'Oh, hello, Sergeant. No, Peter's away I'm afraid.'

'Do you know of anyone else from the Mountain Club that I can talk to?' Douglas Ndhlovu asked. 'Somebody in the area?'

'No, Sergeant, as far as I know, everybody's away. They've all gone up to Mont-aux-Sources on a rescue mission.' Wendy held the phone up and gestured to her guest sitting at the breakfast table. 'Sorry,' she whispered.

'What happened at Mont-aux-Sources?' asked the policeman.

'A German tourist had a heart attack and collapsed. On one of the trails high up.'

'What am I going to do now?' The policeman sounded frustrated.

'Sergeant, what's the problem? Can I perhaps help in some way?' Wendy concentrated as the man spoke. 'What? You say someone's fallen in the Pitseng Pass?'

'Yes, Mrs Wendy.'

'This is unusual - two incidents at the same time! Who is it?'

'It is a woman from Lesotho, Mrs Wendy.'

'Must be one of the drug runners. Is she badly hurt?'

'Yes, ma'am.'

'Oh dear. Sergeant, as I said, there's nobody here,' Wendy went on, 'Peter says that to get the German chap stabilised and then part way down will take all day. Access is very difficult. Then they have to wait for the rescue helicopter which can only get there tomorrow morning. So, at the earliest, Peter will probably only be back tomorrow night.'

56

Wendy thought for a moment. 'How far up the Pitseng Pass is the woman?'

'Near the top. About five or six hours walking, maybe even longer,' Sergeant Ndhlovu replied. 'That's according to one of the victims' accomplices who is with me.'

'Maybe I can go up,' Wendy suggested. 'See what I can do. That is, if you would allow the man who is with you to show me the way.'

'I am not sure about that,' said the policeman dubiously.

'Wait, it's just come to me - I wonder if Garth might be around. I know he's not with Peter and the team at Mont-aux-Sources. Maybe he can help you.'

'I've tried phoning him, but there's no signal at the moment,' Ndhlovu said. 'Maybe the cloud cover is low and too thick.'

'Shall I drive out and see him?' Wendy asked.

'No, Mrs Wendy, that's okay. I'll go.'

'Sergeant, my guest wants to say something. Please hold on for a moment.'

'I could come with you,' the woman said softly. 'I have my hiking boots and proper clothing. I would just need a rucksack, sleeping bag and a small tent. Or I could share?'

Wendy studied her guest carefully. She looked fit enough. 'What about the altitude? It's over three thousand metres above sea level there.'

'I'm used to it. Where I worked was the same height. And I walked everywhere.'

Wendy still looked uncertain.

'Maybe something else will convince you,' her guest said. 'I'm a doctor too, and I have some of my medical kit with me.'

'Did you hear that, Sergeant?' Wendy asked.

'Yes, I got the gist of it.'

'We'll get our kit ready in the meantime,' Wendy said. 'Phone me once you've spoken to Garth. See what he thinks.'

'Okay, Mrs Wendy, thank you. I will be in touch.' The policeman rang off.

***

Out to the east the sun was slowing emerging, an orange hue glowing as the mist in the lower valleys towards Underberg and

Himeville started to burn off. Directly behind Garth's home a blanket of white cloud covered the top of the Drakensberg, concealing the summit of Sani Pass and the Twelve Apostles.

He sat on the veranda, his feet up on the railing. Rusty lay beside him, his soft brown eyes closed in gentle slumber. Garth wondered if the dog felt as tired as he did. He and Rusty had arrived back late the previous evening and they'd only managed a few hours' sleep.

The hiking group he had led along the traverse to Bushman's Nek had been difficult and petulant, often bad-tempered. And unfit as well; it had taken eight full days to walk what normally should have taken just six. For long stretches he had helped carry one of the men's backpacks in addition to his own.

Garth stood and went indoors. The dog's eyes momentarily opened, following his movements, and then they closed again.

The man fired up the gas cooker and filled the kettle. While waiting for the water to boil he took in the main room of his simple home. It hardly seemed possible that he had lived there for more than fifteen years.

The photographs on the walls were what kept him there - mostly images he had taken of the birds of the mountains. The great birds of prey and the great aerial scavengers. Huge bearded vultures and the smaller Cape vultures; black eagles and crowned eagles, rock kestrels, peregrine falcons and the migrating Amur falcons with their distinctive red feet. Some of the images were small, others large; all were stylishly mounted.

A totally different picture hung above the fireplace.

It was a large photographic portrait of a captivating young woman of Asian origin. She was dressed in a high-necked tunic; lustrous black hair hung down to her shoulders and her mouth was set in a radiant smile.

Visitors to his home always commented on the photos of the birds, and even more so on the photo of the woman. But she was the enigma. Garth never spoke of her; he would quietly turn any questions of her aside.

He sighed as he took in her image. Even after all these years the pain he felt was always just below the surface. It never left him.

As if just spoken, her last words to him still burned fresh in his memory. The suddenness of it all, and then the loneliness that followed...

The university holidays were about to begin, their third year studies almost completed.

She was crying when he met her at their favourite spot in the park next to the cricket ground where a huge ancient oak cast wide shadows on the banks of the Dusi River.

He had never seen her like this before. She was always so happy and carefree.

'What is it? What's wrong?' He tried to put his arms around her but she pushed him away gently.

'My parents have forbidden me from seeing you anymore,' she sobbed. 'The Imam has been to our house.'

'But ...'

'They are taking me overseas to finish my degree.'

'When?'

'We fly tomorrow.'

'But they can't do this! You are an adult, not a child anymore. You are nearly twenty-three years old. This is the twenty-first century!'

'You do not understand. This is an honour thing. If I do not do as they say, they...' her melodious, slight husky voice trembled, 'they will have me killed.'

'What?'

'Yes, that is what they will do,' she said, now more assertive.

'Come away with me. We can leave now. My parents will help us; they adore you.'

'Garth, my darling, my love, look over there.' She pointed.

Less than a hundred metres away stood four men, darkly menacing, next to a large SUV.

'My uncles and brother. Waiting for me. They have guns and knives, and unless I go now they will hurt us.'

Garth looked at her helplessly. 'You know...I...I...love you,' he stammered.

'And I love you too. You are buried in my heart. Deep in my soul.' With shaking hands she opened a large carrier bag.

Taking out a carefully wrapped flat rectangular package, she placed it in his hands.

'Take this. Keep it. Wherever you are, I will always be with you.'

***

Garth heard the kettle boiling and turned away to switch it off.

There was a noise outside. Rusty barked once in warning, then went silent. Going to the window, Garth saw a police van coming up the drive.

'Bloody hell, Douglas, I've just returned! And now you want me to go back up again?'

'Garth, what can I do?' The policeman shrugged helplessly. 'You are the only one who can help me. All the others are away.'

'That's okay, I didn't mean to be rude. I'd heard that there was a problem at Mont-aux-Sources.'

'Yes, Wendy says that it may take another day or so to sort out.'

'So tell me about your problem,' Garth sighed.

'Wait I'll call the man in.' The policeman went to the doorway and whistled, gesturing to his junior colleague sitting in the van.

'Bring the *skelm* in here,' he shouted.

Douglas translated the man's account. 'There were three of them,' he said. 'Carrying bales of *dagga* leaves on their heads. You know – you've seen them coming out of Lesotho, down through the narrow passes into South Africa.'

Garth nodded.

'Anyway, this boy here,' Douglas pointed to the poorly clad and clearly frightened youth, 'says the one in the front of him stumbled. The bale on her head slipped and she tried to catch it but the momentum pulled her over the edge and down a cliff.'

'A woman? How far did she fall?'

'It's his sister. The boy is not sure how far she fell. They couldn't see where she landed. Apparently there is some sort of overhang concealing what is below. Personally, I think they were too frightened to look properly.'

'Is the woman alive?' Garth asked.

'He says yes; they could hear her groaning,' Ndhlovu replied.

'So you have this one in custody. Where is the third person?'

'It's his older brother. He's waiting at the point where their sister fell.'

Garth exhaled, then spoke. 'Okay, Rusty and I will head off after breakfast. Please ask this boy what he thinks I'll need to take with me.'

'Thank you. I will ask.' There was a rapid exchange in Sotho. 'The boy says you need ropes and those steel things - what do you call them? Clamps, pegs? And medical things - a stretcher, blankets, splints and so on.'

'Douglas, I am only one man!'

'Wendy said that she will go with you.' The policeman thought for a moment. 'One of her guests, a doctor fortunately, is also prepared to help. And I will let this boy go free. He can also help carry equipment.'

'Wait a bit, Douglas, let's think this through.' Garth unfolded a hiking map. 'Maybe you can drop me here. On the forestry track. That will save at least two hours walking, maybe a bit more. Then do the same for Wendy and her guest.'

The policeman nodded in agreement.

'I'll set off ahead,' Garth said. 'Let this boy go with Wendy to show her the way. That is, if you can trust him.'

'I will give permission for Mrs Wendy to carry a gun. That will keep this rogue in line,' Douglas replied matter-of-factly.

***

Wendy's thoughts were consumed with curiosity as she studied the woman who was walking up ahead. She was like a panther, with a lithe loping walking style, one of Peter's rifles slung over her shoulder as if it belonged there.

Wendy was reminded of the female soldiers she had seen on television. She couldn't remember if they were Kurds or Pathans, but somehow this woman's bearing and poise, the determination in her shoulders and back, looked just the same.

That the woman was striking was without doubt; almost more handsome rather than beautiful. She had high cheekbones, a finely shaped slightly aquiline nose, full sensuous lips and ebony hair cut in a stylish bob.

From her guest register she knew that the woman's first name was Amira, but what Amira was doing there puzzled her; she seemed to be so unusual, so out of place. As they walked, Wendy tried talking to her. Amira was reticent in response.

'Are you on holiday?' Wendy asked.

'I have family in South Africa. I've come to see them,' came the reply.

'But what made you come up here? Into the mountains, into the Drakensberg?'

For a moment there was no reply, then, in a low voice, Amira answered. 'I've wanted to come here for a long time. It is something I need to do. Something to set right.'

Wendy tried to question her further, but Amira was not to be drawn.

They walked on in silence, climbing steadily. The black youth from Lesotho led out in the front, steadily picking his way up the steep rocky path ahead of them. His few words of English were limited to saying how much further they had to go.

Long, dark, menacing shadows stretched down the slopes of the all-encompassing mountains. A light drizzle had begun to fall, the temperature dropping rapidly. A sharp, slippery and treacherous incline brought them to the top of a rocky knoll.

'We here,' the youth said simply.

Another boy emerged from where he had been sheltering in a shallow cave. They exchanged a few hushed words in Sotho. Not moving from the backpack it was guarding, a large russet mountain dog of uncertain parentage and heritage wagged his tail good-naturedly. Two ropes lay across the path in front of them. Both were looped and knotted around a large boulder and then dropped down over what appeared to be an almost sheer precipice.

'Let's take a look and see what's going on,' Wendy said.

The two women offloaded their backpacks and moved closer to the edge. Lying on their stomachs, they peered over.

'My God, look at that,' Wendy whispered, her breath taken away.

They were on top of an overhang, the rock face curving sharply inwards below them. About twenty metres down the face opened out, forming a narrow ledge. Below the ledge was a vertical drop, probably hundreds of metres deep. They couldn't see how far it fell; there was just an enormous dark void.

To the left of where the ropes lay, a narrow curving cleft in the rock face cut down to the ledge below them. Spring-loaded cams tied the ropes back into the cleft.

'Garth must have climbed down there,' said Wendy.

On the ledge they could make out two figures, one clearly dressed in a high visibility jacket crouching over a second.

'Hello-o Garth, we're here!' Wendy shouted. 'Garth, can you hear me?' Her voice echoed back off the surrounding crags.

'Wendy, can you see me?' came the reply.

'Ye-es. Is the woman still alive?'

'She's unconscious. In a bad way. Is the doctor with you?'

'Yes. What do you want us to do?'

'Make camp,' he shouted. 'Pitch tents before the weather closes in.'

'Will do. And what else?'

'Give me another ten minutes or so!'

'Okay!'

The women and boys erected two of the small tents they had brought on an almost level grassy patch. The boys took the third one up to the small cave just above them. They did not pitch the tent, just indicated that they would open it and use it as a blanket of sorts.

Wendy lit a small spirit stove. 'We need to boil water, fill our flasks and make tea,' she said wearily. 'It's going to be a long, cold, damp night.'

When they were finished with their tasks they returned to the cliff's edge.

'Garth, we've made camp,' she called down.

'Good, I'm ready now. Can you see the two ropes hanging in the cleft?'

'Yes.'

'The rope to the right is attached to a harness. Can you pull on it?'

Wendy slid over to it on her stomach. 'This one?' she shouted, tugging on the rope.

'Yes, that's it. I have the woman fixed into a sling and harness. Take your time and lift her up slowly. It's on a belay. Just take it slow and easy.'

In the enclosing gloom, with the rainfall steadily increasing, the women and boys pulled the casualty up. Twenty minutes later they hauled the woman over the edge and dragged her to safety.

While Amira and the two boys untied the woman and moved her into one of the tents, Wendy went back to the precipice.

'Garth, we've got her secure!'

The mist was getting thicker, the sky murky, nearly dark. Wendy could just make out his shape in the beam of her torchlight.

'I can't get back up now,' he shouted. 'It's too wet, too dark, too dangerous!'

'What do you want us to do then?'

'Use one of the ropes. Wrap some rations and extra clothing in a sleeping bag and groundsheet, then lower it back down to me. Oh, and a torch too, please!'

'Okay, I won't be a moment.'

Slightly suspicious, the dog watched intently as Wendy opened Garth's backpack and put the bundle together for him. In addition to the items he had asked for she added a flask of hot, sweet tea.

'Garth, I'm sending it down now,' she called.

'Thank you, Wendy.' His voice sounded suppressed and muffled. 'I'll see you in the morning. Remember, don't move around till daylight. Stay tight and safe.'

'Okay, Garth, you too!'

**

Amira crept into the tent. Wendy was already tucked deep into her sleeping bag, the rifle close at hand.

'How is she?' Wendy asked.

'She's in a bad way,' replied Amira. 'She must have fallen down that narrow cleft. Her back is badly lacerated and there may be damage to her spine. One arm is broken and her right Achilles could be torn. She's still unconscious.'

'Will she survive?'

'It's difficult to tell. I think she may have a head injury as well.'

'Is there anything else we can do?' asked Wendy, concerned.

'I've cleaned her up and strapped the break,' said Amira. 'And I've got her on a drip. We'll just have to wait and see. I'll check on her through the night.'

Wendy rolled on to her side and was just drifting off to sleep when she heard Amira whisper softly. 'Wendy, is Garth's surname Cruickshanks?'

'Yes,' she replied drowsily.

***

When Wendy awoke, the position where her companion had been sleeping was vacant. Even her bedding was gone.

I wonder where she is? was her first thought, followed by, *And how did she know Garth's name?*

Suddenly worried, Wendy scrambled into her jeans and pulled on her boots. She shivered; her clothes were still very wet from the day before. Outside it was already getting light. The rain had stopped and the sky, although clearing, was still more grey than blue.

Amira was sitting outside the tent where the injured woman lay, half wrapped in her sleeping bag. Curled up under a loose corner, the dog rested comfortably next to her.

'Did you sleep there last night?' Wendy asked.

'Yes. I was concerned about disturbing you all the time so I stayed with the patient. I also heard a strange noise; it woke me up.'

'What noise?'

'I don't know. Sounded like a rumble - perhaps thunder. Or a tremor. Really can't be sure.'

'How is the woman?'

'Very weak, but stable. I don't know how, but we will need to get her to hospital today.'

Wendy nodded. 'Let's go and hear what Garth is going to do.'

The two women crept closer to the edge. They couldn't see a thing. A sea of snowy cloud was spread below them, less than five metres down from where they lay.

'Garth, Ga…arth, can you hear me?' Wendy called.

There was no response.

Wendy shouted again. Still no response.

'I don't think he can hear us,' Amira said. 'I think the mist and clouds are too dense.'

'We'll have to wait for it to break up.' Wendy looked at her watch.

'Can we not phone from higher up?' Amira asked. 'We need more help.'

'Hmmm…' Wendy looked at her watch again. 'It's just 7am. Let's have something to eat and drink and then I'll head on.'

'You can't go alone.'

'No, I'll take one of the boys. The other can stay with you.'

She stood and walked up to the little cave where the two youths were huddled. Taking her mobile phone out of her anorak pocket, she asked where she could call from.

The older boy pointed to a high buttress. 'On side,' he said, holding out his right hand. 'Sometimes signal. We go. I show you.'

Wendy went back to Amira. 'I think it's a solid hour's walk each way. You stay here with your patient. I'll take the rifle but I'll leave you with this.' From beneath her jacket she withdrew a heavy, bulky revolver. 'Do you know how to use this?' she asked.

'Of course,' Amira replied. 'It's a Colt 44 Magnum. Very unusual weapon for a woman.'

Wendy concealed her surprise. *This really is a puzzle. How would she know about a weapon like this?* 'It's not mine,' she told Amira. 'It was given to my husband by an American climber; he's had it for years. I should be back by ten o'clock at the latest. Hopefully the mist will have cleared by then and Garth can get back up. Remember, whatever you do, don't leave this spot.'

'I know what to do,' Amira said quietly.

Over the past few years she had had so many conflicting thoughts, yet her mind was now at peace.

Amira was calm, knew what she was doing. She had come to try and rectify the wrong her parents and uncles had done. But the uncertainty, the turmoil, was created by worrying how Garth would react. So much time had passed by. Maybe he had married somebody else or lived with someone. Perhaps he even had children.

It seemed from her assessment of the situation that he was still a single man, but maybe there were ties that he had somewhere. Had he got over what had been between them, or had he perhaps become bitter because of it? Despite the unanswered questions she was resolute. She still loved him. Never for a day had she not remembered him, not thought of him. She had come to tell him that. Come to tell him that if he still wanted her, she had returned to be with him.

She was in control of her own life now.

The solitary life she had led all these years was over. Her medical work with the Kashmiri people who lived in the high, remote Hindu Kush was over. The difficult and dangerous life, trekking from village to village with just one or two guards, was over. Fending off marriage proposals from ageing warlords was over. Handling and treating wounded Taliban and Al-Qaeda fighters was over. Dealing with arrogant Pashtun Lotharios was over.

She wanted to be with Garth, the soft-spoken, strong and upright young man who had loved her beyond race and tribal boundaries. Loved her without prejudice or possessiveness.

The thoughts tumbled through her head. How ironic it was that they had both retreated to the mountains to forge their individual lives. What was the significance of that? And now the coincidence of them both being here. What were the odds on that?

Amira knew from Garth's guiding website that he lived in this area. That was how she had traced him once she made up her mind to return to South Africa. She had originally planned to contact him from Wendy's Guesthouse and try to arrange to meet him somewhere, but the current events had changed all that.

Once the mist in the valleys was gone Garth would be able to climb back up.

She would be there. Waiting for him. It had to be their destiny.

***

Wendy looked flushed and tired when she arrived back. 'I'm getting too fat and heavy for this type of thing,' she muttered.

'Did you manage to contact someone?' Amira asked.

'Yes, but I could only get through to the border post at the top of Sani Pass. They were surprised to hear from me,' she went on, 'because they were expecting Douglas to ring them with an update.'

'And?'

'They are going to phone Douglas and my husband, and tell them what's going on.'

'What about help?'

'Apparently there are some shepherds nearby. If Douglas allows them to cross into South Africa without papers or passports they will come and help us carry the woman down. I said that we would give them some money too if necessary.'

'How far away are they?' Amira asked.

'They are at Masubasuba now,' Wendy replied. 'Probably six or seven kilometres away. I would think it will take them about four hours or so to get here, probably less. They can move so quickly in this terrain.'

Amira looked worried, pensive. 'Let's hope the policeman gives his permission. I don't think the injured woman will survive much longer without full and proper medical care.'

'We'll have to just wait and see,' Wendy said. 'At least the cloud and mist is starting to break up. Give it another hour or so and let's try and talk to Garth.'

They couldn't see him.

The sky had finally cleared. Apricot sunlight now streamed across the rock faces and gorges. A light breeze blew scented heather across the top of the knoll. Catching an early thermal, a huge bearded vulture glided low overhead. But Garth was gone.

Over and over Wendy shouted, 'Garth, Garth!' Her voice was hoarse and harsh with the effort. There was no response.

Shocked and frightened, the two women crept back from the ledge. For a while neither of them spoke.

'What...what are we going to do now?' Wendy trembled, she seemed close to tears.

Amira took her hand. 'Get the boys to help, please.'

'To do what?'

'To form an anchor to hold me.'

'Hold you?'

68

'Yes. The three of you must hold me - around my legs and ankles.'

'What? Why?'

'I want to hang over the edge. Try and have a better look.'

'But that's madness. You're crazy!'

'We have to do something. We have to know!' There was a raw, desperate emotion in Amira's voice that could not be disguised.

Wendy looked at her sharply. Before she could say anything Amira was already on her feet and calling the boys over.

Carefully they inched forward until her upper body disappeared over the edge.

'A little bit more. Hold tight!' she called. After about twenty seconds she shouted up again, 'Okay, you can pull me up now.'

Amira took a deep breath to regain her composure. 'I think I can see what happened,' she said.

'What?' Wendy asked nervously.

'That noise I heard in the night - remember, the noise that woke me up?'

'Yes.'

'There must have been a rockfall in that crevice where the woman fell down and where the ropes are hanging down. We need to examine the ropes.'

Together they pulled on the first rope. It was loose. Looping it overhand, they lifted it up.

'Look,' Wendy said. 'It's been cut.'

Amira studied it carefully. 'No, I think it's chafed through. See these strands - it looks like rocks have damaged it.'

The second rope was taut and tight. They tried to pull on it but it wouldn't move. Even with the two youths helping they still couldn't budge it.

'Garth must be there,' Wendy said shakily. 'He must be.'

'From what I could see,' Amira said, 'the ledge he was on must have been hit by the rockfall. There seems to be only a small piece of it left. Maybe,' she indicated with her hands, 'a metre or so long and very narrow.'

'Do you think he's underneath it?' Wendy asked. 'Still tied to the rope?'

'Yes, I think so. But I couldn't see him at all.'

69

'Why can't we pull him up then? Even a little.'

'Because there's another problem,' Amira said grimly.

'What is it?'

'Some large rocks seemed to have trapped the rope. It's stuck or caught up in some way.'

'So…' Wendy paused, 'Gareth might be hanging lower down then.'

'Yes, I think so. And he cannot move.'

'I'm going to go down that crevice to the ledge,' Amira said softly. 'Will you help me, please?'

'No, that's impossible!' Wendy replied sternly, 'Don't even consider it, it's far too difficult!'

'I'm going to try. I think the rockfall has widened the crevice a little.' Amira sounded determined. 'I have to try. Help me tie this sling and harness on to the loose rope.' She gathered the gear together and laid it on the ground.

Stunned, Wendy looked at her. And then something flashed through her mind. 'There…there is a picture on a wall in Garth's house,' she said hesitantly '…of a young woman. That's you, isn't it? In fact, I'm sure it's you. That's how you know his surname.'

Amira nodded slightly, but remained silent.

'Just the hair is different. You wear it short now,' Wendy stated.

'Yes.'

'You know, and I'm not quite sure how to say this, there has been no-one else for him. He has always been alone. Not miserable or morbid, just comfortable with himself. Only one of his dogs for company.' Wendy shrugged her shoulders helplessly. 'I really don't know why I'm telling you this now and in this situation, but he's a really good man – he will help anyone, has time for anyone. He's the most decent human being I know.'

'I know. My family did him a great wrong,' Amira said simply. 'I did him a great wrong.'

'And now you're trying to fix that? By doing something incredibly dangerous, something you've never done before?'

'Yes, I have to. I can get down if I'm tied to this sling.' Amira's voice was now even more resolute. 'The three of you can lower me slowly, like one step, one small movement at a time.'

'We need to wait for the Mountain Club people, Amira. We can't deal with this!' Wendy said sharply.

'Look at the ropes, Wendy. I don't think there is much time.' Amira's tone was steely in response. 'If Garth says he is safe and can wait then you can drag me back up, but I must try!'

The rhythm of her descent was awkward. In some places she was able to descend a step or two quite easily, then a loose rock or her inability to find a secure foothold would slow her up.

Amira was determined not to look down. She just kept focusing on her position in the crevice, trying to breathe as she had once been taught in yoga classes.

Each time she shouted they would lower her a little more. The leather gloves that Wendy had lent Amira were quickly abandoned; she couldn't feel for the cracks and holds with them on. But her hands were really taking a battering, and within minutes they were scraped and bleeding, fingernails torn. She remembered reading somewhere that climbers used chalk powder for their hands; now she understood why.

Looking up she could see that she'd descended about fifteen metres. *Maybe only five metres to go*, she thought. *I hope the rope is long enough.*

Slowly and steadily she inched downwards. The sling around her body seemed to have shifted and was now abrasively uncomfortable between her legs. She could do nothing to adjust it until she was on firmer footing.

'A little more,' she whispered. 'Just a little more.'

'There's only a metre of rope left,' Wendy called. 'Are you nearly there?'

'I will need to look down,' Amira whimpered. 'I must be brave.'

She extended her legs.

Suddenly, heart-stoppingly, she lost her balance, swung free and loose, then lost her grip too. Swinging back towards the cliff, she hit the rocks, bouncing once and then again. A sharp edge scraped her forehead. Her hands scrabbled desperately as she clawed back towards the rock surface.

Breathless and unnerved, heart pumping wildly, she forced herself to calm down.

Slowly her breath steadied. Cautiously and very deliberately she looked down.

The ledge was immediately below her. She moved slightly to her right and stretched. Her toes just touched.

'Drop a little,' she shouted up to Wendy.

The sling and harness loosened a fraction and she fell into an unsteady crouch on the ledge. Amira closed her eyes and breathed deeply, trying to slow her heart rate. She had never been as scared as this. Making sure she was settled properly, she tried to ease the cramp in her legs and wipe away the blood that was trickling into her eyes. Then she opened them.

She gazed around. The void facing her was immense. Like a huge magnet, it seemed to draw her in. The security of being tied to the rope and sling was the only thing that prevented her from fainting into vertigo.

Turning to face the crevice she had just come down, she saw an ice axe wedged into a small crack in the rock face to her left. Attached to it was a water bottle, a torch and a short length of thin rope. She drew the bottle to her lips and took a sip. Fear had made her so thirsty. Despite wanting to drink more, she forced herself to stop.

Gathering her breath, she gasped weakly, 'Garth,' then a little louder, 'Garth.' Suddenly a demonic, powerful charge filled her. 'Garth!' Her voice echoed, dying away across the vast gorge.

'Garth!' she screamed again.

For a moment all was still. Then, as if from some other world, came a strained, 'Who, who…is…that?'

'He's alive. Praise Allah,' she whimpered, her years of religious indifference immediately forgotten. 'Garth, it's Amira!'

'Who?'

'Garth, it's me, Amira. I'm here.'

'Amira? Amira Khan?' Tortured as his voice was, she could hear the disbelief.

'Yes, it's me!'

'Where are you?'

'On the ledge. I think just above you.'

'I can't believe it. What are you doing here? Are you safe? Secure?'

'Yes, I am safe. You must tell me what to do to help you.'

'Amira, please, you must be very careful. This is a bad situation.' His voice seemed stronger now.

'I'm okay, Garth. I'm tied on firmly.'

'Amira, are you okay?' Wendy called down, her voice fraught. 'Can you see Garth? Is he alive?'

'No, I can't see him but we are talking.'

'That's great! Just shout when you need me to do something!'

'Sorry, Garth, I was just talking to Wendy.' Amira said. 'Tell me what to do.'

'Amira, my left hand must be trapped under a large rock. Can you see it?'

She looked to where the ledge had been damaged by the rockfall and edged slightly closer. Carefully she scraped a few smaller stones and some scree to one side. The ends of his fingers now lay exposed, bunched together. All appeared bloody and broken, the middle finger trapped across the top of the others. A large square chunk of rock lay across the top of his hand. Amira tried to shift it but the rock wouldn't budge.

'I can't move it!' she shouted.

'Use the ice axe. Like a lever.'

Even when she used the tool, the rock still would not give way.

'Sorry, Garth, it's too heavy. It's jammed tight!'

'Amira, we have to free my hand!' he shouted now. 'My left shoulder is also dislocated, maybe even broken!'

'I'm trying, Garth, I'm trying!'

'If I can get my hand free I'll be able to swing around - use my right hand to belay back up. Or use the ice axe to pull myself up.'

'Where are you? How far down?' Amira asked. 'I can't see you.'

'I'm just under the ledge, right below you. But with my whole left side out of action, it may as well be a hundred metres down!'

'Let me try again!' she shouted desperately.

Amira lay on the ledge and tried to push the rock with her feet. Nothing happened. Jamming the head of the ice axe as far

73

under the rock as it would go, she pushed as hard as she could. Still nothing happened.

Weeping at her futility, she stopped. 'Garth, I just can't move it!'

A few seconds passed, then a few more. Neither of them said anything.

Garth spoke next. 'Amira, you know what to do. Just do it,' he said brutally.

'What?' Like a bolt between the eyes the realisation of what he was saying hit her. 'Garth, I can't do that,' she wailed.

'Amira, take the axe and do it.'

'I can't!'

'Amira, listen to me. The rope below the ledge is fraying, shredding. If it goes, how long will my torn shoulder hold? And I can't feel my fingers or my hand. We have so little time. Please just do it!'

'Oh, Garth, I just can't!'

'Amira, why are you here?'

'I...I came to find you. To say sorry. To tell you how much...I have missed you,' she said brokenly. 'To tell you...that I still love you.'

'Do you want to be with me? Live with me forever?'

'Yes, yes, of course!'

'Then you have no choice.' His voice was calm now, and very gentle. She could hardly hear him. 'I'm here, my darling, just waiting to be with you again. I have never stopped loving you.'

Sobbing, Amira cleared the area around his hand a little more. As best as she could, she pressed his mangled fingers closer together.

'I will only try once,' she whispered to herself.

Bracing herself as securely as she could, she took a deep breath and lifted the ice axe high above her head. Exhaling slowly, she closed one eye, focussed the other and aimed for the top of his middle finger.

Contracting her stomach muscles, she swung the axe down in a fluid, sweeping blow.

***

The bronze plaques are mounted on the side of a huge boulder near the top of Pitseng Pass.

Twice a year Wendy makes the long hike up to them. It is something she has to do. It's not that she wants to relive that fateful, terrible day, or hurt herself emotionally anymore; she finds the journey rehabilitating, the cleaning and polishing of the plaques cathartic.

On the larger tablet there is an engraving of two eagles flying. The inscription reads:

THIS STONE REMAINS THEIR MONUMENT
Amira Khan   Garth Cruickshanks
1979 – 2018   1978 – 2018
'In balance with our lives, our love is where eagles soar.'

Wendy was lying on her stomach looking over the precipice when she saw Garth heave his chest and right shoulder on to the ledge. In that instant the rope must have snapped. Without a sound he fell back out of sight into the boundless, impenetrable depths below.

Frozen and shocked, Wendy heard Amira scream. It was a prolonged shriek of pure, terrible anguish, the likes of which she had never heard before and had never heard since. The sound pierced her innermost psyche.

Not believing what she was seeing, Wendy observed Amira stand shakily and remove the harness and sling, watched as Amira moved to the edge of the ledge.

Stricken, unable to make a sound, she saw Amira raise her arms as if in surrender and then, with a flying leap, throw herself down into the abyss after Garth.

Wendy always cries openly when she polishes the smaller plaque.

Rusty Cruickshanks
2018
'His love was like theirs - total.'

After the events of that dreadful day she had taken Rusty the mountain dog home with her. Three days later he disappeared.

For some months shepherds had reported seeing him in the Pitseng foothills searching for the master he had lost. 'Like a wind ghost,' they said. His forlorn, sorrow-filled howling resounded through the valleys.

Then the reports ended.

Wendy believed that Rusty finally found Garth and had laid down next to his remains for eternity.

Rusty's body and those of Garth and Amira, the woman whose love for Garth had been equally as deep and absolute, have never been discovered.

CRICKETER

South Africa 2017

The three boys stood on the footbridge that crossed over the motorway. They giggled uncontrollably as they watched the cars and trucks passing beneath them.

They were high, eyes stoned to bloodshot orbs in their sockets. The glue pot they had inhaled from and the two large bottles of stolen cough mixture they had consumed now lay empty and smashed on the tarmac below.

The youngest had a facebrick in his hands. It weighed nearly three kilograms. In his drugged condition he could only just manage to lift it up to the parapet of the bridge.

'*Wag, ek sal jou sê*. Wait, wait, I'll tell you when,' one of the older boys screamed wildly. 'Five, four, three, two, one. *Fok*, now! Bombs away!'

The boy dropped the brick.

***

It was one of those fine balmy evenings in March. Warm, with a light sea breeze filtering in from the Atlantic Ocean. The black outline of Table Mountain was visibly defined in the clear night sky.

The two women walked along the upmarket Waterfront. Along with the early throngs of well-heeled tourists and exuberant locals, they admired the window displays.

They spent most of their time in front of the ornate jewellery shops. The intricate beautiful gold and silver items made them pause, look twice. There was a specific ring that one of them particularly liked.

'Look, Hendie,' she exclaimed. 'Isn't that ring amazing?' She pointed to a stunningly cut rose-hued diamond set in a wide band of solid gold. 'Oh, I wish there was a man for me. A man who would want me to wear it for him.'

Her friend Hendrina, or Hendie as she was known to all, just laughed. 'Where will you meet a man who can afford something like that? We are just two waifs, two orphans in our twenties. We'll be lucky just to find proper boyfriends. And then we'll probably have to support them!'

'Oh, Hendie, you are right. You are always right,' Rachel sighed. 'But we can dream, can't we?'

They linked arms and strolled on. They weren't sisters, they were closer than that. They were closer than twins. Inseparable. Their roots were deep and entwined.

They had grown up together from the age of seven. Hendie was an abandoned child. Rachel, whose parents had been killed, had no other family to speak of that would take care of her.

The orphanage in which they had been placed was shabby and under-funded, with lax discipline. The two little girls had clung together, always looking out for each other. Their schooling had been average with no academic achievements of note, but both had become good sportswomen. Hendie was close to being selected for the national hockey team, with Rachel not far behind.

The provincial coach had helped a lot, obtaining access for them to college where both had qualified - one as a dental technician, the other as a physiotherapist.

'I got paid today,' Hendie said. 'Shall we get something to eat and drink?'

The Sportsman's Place was lively but not yet full. A recorded English Premier League football match blared from the television screens in the bar area.

Hendie and Rachel chose to sit outside on the deck, the sea lapping across the rocks below them. They talked quietly, watching the gulls feeding on the small fish in the grey ocean water. When their food came they both ate slowly and carefully, an appreciation learnt after many years of small, poorly prepared meals.

There was a sudden flurry of guests, a large group of men all arriving at the same time.

'It's the South African cricket team,' Hendie whispered in an awed voice. 'I heard they were in Cape Town preparing for the one-day series against Sri Lanka. I think the first match is on Saturday.'

The men were boisterous, but not overly so. They settled down at the tables nearby, sitting in groups of three and four. Even though they sat at various separate tables they talked across to one another, laughing at the jokes and light-hearted banter. They were clearly a happy and well-bonded team.

'Let's order a dessert,' Hendie grinned. 'Stretch it out. Maybe one or two will come and talk to us.'

'Oh, Hendie, these guys move in different circles to us,' Rachel muttered.

***

Hendie was incorrigible. Rachel watched as she gave the guys the eye, subtly flirting with the two men closest to them.

'Hendie, stop it,' Rachel said, 'I know what you're doing. They're probably married!'

'No rings. I've already looked!'

It didn't take long before one of the men stretched across to them. 'Would you like to join us?' he asked politely. 'Or can we sit with you? We've been with this lot all day.' He gestured to the fourteen other men spread around the restaurant. 'We really need a change of scenery.'

Hendie smiled happily and, with a shuffling of chairs, the two men joined them.

'My name is Tyrone. Please call me Ty, everyone does. And this is Adrian.'

They sat and chatted easily. Ty was a natural wit and imitator, but all within bounds. He soon had them chuckling at the antics and quirks of his team mates. He was clever and erudite and had obviously been well educated. They later discovered that he'd completed a degree in Physics at the University of Cape Town. And now he was studying part-time for his Masters in the same subject.

A smitten Hendie subtly moved closer to him.

After a while Rachel found herself talking quietly to Adrian. He was self-possessed and reserved, considered in his responses.

'Ty is helping me,' he said softly. 'I'm the new boy in the team. He's sort of looking out for me.'

'Have you played for South Africa yet?' Rachel asked.

'Only at under nineteen level,' he replied. 'And for the A side.'

'And do you think you'll play this weekend?'

'It will be an honour if I'm selected.'

Ty overheard the conversation. 'This man is one of our most talented players,' he stated.

'Really?'

'Yes. He will be playing for South Africa for many years to come.'

'Ty, you're exaggerating,' Adrian said quietly.

'Man, you know you're good. You are also the fittest and have a great eye. And do you know what, ladies?'

'What?' Rachel asked.

'He's very good at other sports too. Racket sports like badminton, but he's even better at squash. He would be a pro if there was any money in the game.'

'How did you get so good?' Rachel asked.

Adrian looked down; it seemed he could not face her as he replied. 'It's a long story. Maybe for another day.'

For a moment everyone was silent. Around the restaurant their team mates were standing up.

'We have to go now, Hendie and Rachel,' Ty said. 'Voluntary curfew,' he laughed. 'We have to be back at the hotel by 11pm so we're fresh for practice tomorrow morning.'

He shook their hands and looked thoughtful. 'Would you like to come to the match on Saturday? As our guests?'

Hendie held on to his hand and spontaneously hugged him.

Ty placed his hands gently on her shoulders. 'That's for another day too,' he said.

***

That Saturday at the test match would define their lives forever.

Both men played well. Adrian scored an attractive half century before being run out by his batting partner. Later in the innings Ty hit the winning runs with a powerful lofted on-drive for six. But for the two women the day was more than that. Hendie and Ty were on a fast track to a long and happy marriage.

Rachel and Adrian were headed for rough ground.

***

80

Rachel watched as Hendie quickly grew into her relationship with Ty. When the couple were together their joy in each other was unbounded. Their happiness permeated all who knew them.

They had all the technology needed to stay in touch when the South African team was away on tour - various apps on their mobile phones, Instagram, Facebook, Skype and email. Each of them also had a satellite phone.

When the team was playing in South Africa, Hendie would attend every match that she could. In the glow of her support, Ty's game became even better and more unfettered.

With Rachel and Adrian it was different.

She fell in love with him slowly. She did not know why that was, could not quite put her finger on it. Perhaps because Adrian was shyer and more introverted. His deep focus on improvement and fitness made him less spontaneous than she would have wanted. But he did adore her.

Hendie was always confirming it. 'He talks to Ty,' Hendie said, 'about how beautiful you are. How calm and at peace with the world you are. That you are someone beyond his wildest dreams. He says to Ty that you are more important to him than his sport, his career.' At the time Hendie had looked at Rachel, her voice very serious. 'Adrian is deep, very deep. There are things hidden away. Who knows what they are. But you are good for him and he is good for you.'

***

It took Rachel a while to understand Adrian. She later realised that, in fact, she had not even come close. Sometimes she watched him as he trained. Hour after hour he batted in the nets or in practice games. He would wear out the bowling coach, then carry on facing the bowling machine.

When his teammates were done for the day Adrian still was not finished. He would continue working on his fielding and catching or strength and resistance training in the gym. Other times he played ferocious squash matches against the best opponents in the area.

She steadily came to live with his drive and determination. Where the root of it lay, where it all came from, was still beyond her.

When they were not in camp, the players received training and nutritional schedules from the SA team's coaches. Adrian always did more, needed more.

The head coach made a point of discussing the schedules with Rachel. Sometimes he saw her at the practices, other times he would phone her to go over them. Between them they planned Adrian's life.

Sometimes Rachel thought that it was a little unhealthy, but the head coach convinced her otherwise. This new role steadily gave her an important sense of value.

But the area that Rachel could not penetrate was Adrian's past. He refused to speak of it.

Whenever she broached the subject he would gently take her hand and say, 'My life started when I was about eight. Before that - nothing. A man found me. A sportsman; more than a sportsman really. And he saved me and cared for me, just as you are now doing.' His soft voice would quiver slightly and he would not be drawn any further.

Their lives drew closer. After a while they rented a bigger apartment and started furnishing it with items they both liked. On the day of Hendie and Ty's wedding Adrian gave Rachel a ring - the beautiful gold and diamond band Rachel had so admired on the evening they first met.

Adrian was doing well, with a permanent place in the South African team. He had a well-paid contract and an agent whom they both liked and trusted. Significant sponsorship deals had been secured.

Their domestic horizon looked clear and fine.

The early summer's day was glorious. A light cover of wispy white cloud lay over Table Mountain and, ahead to their left, clouds stretched along the tops of the Franschoek Mountains.

Rachel and Adrian were on their way to Somerset West, some forty-five kilometres from Cape Town. Adrian and other members of the South African team were to attend a mini-cricket festival there.

Rachel always enjoyed these days out, watching the excited little boys and girls interacting with their heroes. Their enthusiasm was contagious and surged through her as well. Sometimes she even joined in their boisterous games, enjoying the children's spontaneity which was absent in her years of survival in the orphanage.

They drove out of Cape Town and made their way through Bellville. The motorway was relatively quiet, traffic flowing smoothly in each direction.

They had decided to buy a house and were discussing their plans, including the areas they had seen. Adrian was very enthusiastic. 'We must have our own gym. And a sauna. Maybe even a lap pool.' He had reason to be excited; the money he was now earning made their lives really comfortable. The dreams for their own home were close to realisation.

Steadily Adrian picked up speed. The vast impoverished areas of the Cape Flats lay on either side of the road and the Khayelitsha slums loomed up ahead. Turning his head, he saw that Rachel had gone still, looked a little pale.

'Is something wrong?' he asked.

'I don't like talking about it, but we are near to where my parents were killed.' She hesitated before continuing. 'I told you they died in a car accident, but this is the first time that we have been past here together.'

'What happened exactly?'

'You see that footbridge?' Rachel pointed ahead.

'Yes.'

'Someone dropped a brick. It caused my father to have an accident.'

'When?' Adrian asked quietly.

'October, seventeen years ago.'

Neither of them said anything more. Like a slow-moving dense sea-fog, an impervious, sad atmosphere seemed to descend and engulf them. Rachel reached across to touch Adrian. The tension within him was palpable.

At the next exit he took the off-ramp, turned the car around and started heading back to Cape Town.

'What are you doing?' Rachel asked.

'I need to take you back home.'

'What? Now?'

'Yes, there is something I need to do.' Adrian's voice was strained, his face pale and taut, white-lipped.

'But the cricket? Your participation?'

'I'll phone the organiser and explain.'

'Explain what?'

Adrian did not reply. He gazed straight ahead. Drove faster, hands rigid on the steering wheel. Ten minutes later he dropped her off.

'Adrian?'

He just shook his head. 'I must go.'

'Please Adrian, please phone me when you've done whatever you've forgotten to do,' she pleaded. Bewildered and hurt, she watched as he drove away. Her mind churned. Whatever had gotten into him?

***

Rachel could not sleep. She lay awake all night. There had been no word from Adrian. She tried phoning him. Over and over. His phone appeared to be switched off.

The worry was beyond her understanding. She shook continuously; her mind and body felt bound in ice, trapped in uncertainty, then in torpor. She looked at her watch again. Four o'clock. Making her way to the kitchen, she filled the kettle.

Suddenly the doorbell rang. Her heart seemed to stop.

Hendie and Tyrone were at the door; they looked distraught. Hendie had clearly been crying - her eyes were red, face smudged and blotchy. Next to her Tyrone's expression was grim and grey and bleak.

'Rachel,' he said shakily. 'Rachel, we need to come in. We're sorry it's so early.'

'Of course, of course,' her eyes took in their distress. Saw the shock. 'Oh my God, Adrian,' she whispered. 'Something's happened.'

She could feel all strength leave her and she started to sway and crumple.

Ty caught her as she fell. Lifting Rachel, he carried her into the lounge. Hendie coaxed her onto the couch, sat close and wrapped her arms around her.

'What's happened, Hendie? Where's Adrian?' Rachel asked desperately.

But her dearest and closest friend could not speak. Choked up, tears streamed down her cheeks. She took one of Rachel's hands; Tyrone held the other.

Tyrone tried to clear his throat. He coughed, took a deep breath and began. 'Rachel…Adrian is gone.'

'Gone? Gone where?'

'Rachel…' he stammered, 'Rachel…he is dead.'

'Dead?' She looked wildly from one to the other.

'Yes.'

Hendie nodded numbly in agreement; still could not speak.

'It can't be true! Tell me it's not true. That…that it's just a rumour. Or that he's just gone missing!'

'No, Rachel, we can't. It's true.' Ty could not contain himself any longer. He dropped his head down to his hands and covered his face, back and shoulders shaking as he wept.

'What happened? Was it a car accident?'

Ty looked up. 'No, Rachel.' He tried to gather himself. 'No, Rachel, he…he…' The words struggled to come out. 'He…committed suicide.'

'Never!' Rachel screamed. She tried to lash out at Ty.

Hendie held her tightly. 'We love you.' Her voice was barely audible. 'Let Ty finish.'

'The police found him last night. Just after eleven o'clock.' Ty spoke haltingly. 'It took a while for them to work out who the victim was.'

'Why? Why?' Rachel cried.

'Let Tyrone carry on,' Hendie said soothingly.

'Once they knew, they got hold of Coach. He's in Johannesburg for a meeting.'

'Why didn't the police come directly to me? This doesn't sound right. What is going on?'

'The police were being circumspect,' Tyrone said. 'They were thinking of the South African cricket team and all that it means to our country. Adrian, as you know, was becoming our star player. A future world star.'

'What happened next?' Rachel whispered.

'Coach phoned me. He knows we are all close.'

'When?'

'About two hours ago. He…he wanted to catch the first flight to Cape Town this morning.'

'Why?'

'To come and tell you himself. But I told him that Hendie and I would do it.'

'Why only now if you knew two hours ago?' Rachel whimpered. 'You're only ten minutes away. Why didn't you come and see me sooner?'

'Because we had to wait for the police to…brief us. Tell us what happened.'

'And?'

Overwhelmed, Tyrone shook his head.

'Hendie, how did he die?' Rachel screamed. 'Please, I need to know!'

Hendie was equally overwrought; could not speak. She buried her head tight into Rachel's shoulder.

Slowly Ty gathered himself. He opened Hendie's handbag and took out a cream-coloured envelope.

'Adrian…Adrian left this…for you.' He handed it over. 'Maybe there's an explanation.'

With quivering hands she opened it, unfolded the note inside. Adrian's writing was as she knew it, the words neat, letters carefully formed:

Rachel, my one and only ever love,

I adore and worship you.

Seventeen years ago, on 11 October 2000, I dropped the brick that caused the accident in which your parents were killed. I saw what I did. And I saw what happened.

The damage I have done to you is beyond forgiveness.
I do not deserve to live.

Adrian

Numbly she read the brief note again, gave it to Hendie. She and Ty read it together. Hendie was the first to speak. 'It can't be...' She started to cry again.

Rachel's eyes were frenzied. 'Now you have to tell me, Ty. You have to! How did Adrian die?'

'Please, Rachel,' he implored. 'Please...it's too terrible. I don't know how...how to tell you.'

'How much worse can it get?' Her voice was shrill and uncontrolled. 'How much worse?'

'He drove out to Cape Point. Found a deserted parking area and...' He couldn't continue.

Hendie took his hand. 'Tell her, my darling,' she said comfortingly.

Ty looked stricken. 'He left his car. With your letter on the seat.'

'And?' Rachel's eyes bored into him, her tears enhancing the ferocious enquiry within them.

'He went to sit on a bench. You know, one of those benches that overlook the sea.'

'And?'

Ty struggled to find the words. 'He...he immolated himself.'

'What? What do you mean?' she shrieked.

'He...he poured petrol over himself.'

'Oh, no!'

'Yes,' Tyrone was crying openly now. The image in his mind was so terrible and appalling. 'Yes. Then he lit a match.'

'And?'

'That was it.'

'Did anyone see him? Try to stop him?' Rachel's tone was shocked and broken.

'There were some men. Homeless people sleeping rough. Some way away, in the bushes,' Ty replied shakily. 'By the time they realised what was happening, heard...heard Adrian screaming, it was far too late...' His voice tailed off.

For a while none of them spoke. Hendie and Ty held Rachel in their arms. They could feel her trembling uncontrollably.

Then she went still, eerily calm. 'Do you know why he...he killed himself like that?' she whispered.

'No,' Hendie murmured back. 'We are completely mystified.' Something struck her. 'Do you know?'

'Yes. Read his letter again. The second paragraph. The last sentence.'

Hendie opened the folded note again, read out aloud. '*And I saw what happened.*'

'Yes. My mother and father were gardeners, contractors, on their way to a client. I was at school.' Rachel shuddered and drew a deep breath. 'My father had two drums of petrol in the back of his van. For the lawnmowers.'

Hendie had her hand to her mouth. Ty already anticipated Rachel's next words.

'When the brick smashed the windscreen, they veered to the side and hit another car. Then a big truck hit them. There were sparks.'

As if all the air had been sucked from the room, Ty tried to speak, to interrupt, to stop her, but could not.

Her voice unrelenting and dead, Rachel continued. 'In the ensuing inferno, my parents were burnt to death. And that is why Adrian did what he did.'

THE RECCE

England 2002

She watched as her class settled down. It was the last lesson of the week and the pupils were lively and exuberant, gearing up for the weekend ahead. The boys were especially high-spirited with their buzzcut-styled hair and baggy school trousers. She knew that appearances made little difference; some of them were very bright and creative as well.

She enjoyed teaching them and they enjoyed her lessons.

'Kate?' The head teacher stood in the doorway, beckoning, a worried look on his normally bland face. She went to the door.

He drew her into the passage and spoke quietly but anxiously. 'Kate, there are two police officers in my office. They would like to have a word with you.'

'The police? What do they want?'

'I have no idea. They say it's a confidential matter.'

'What about my class?'

'I'll look after them until you return,' he replied.

'What will you do?'

'I'll do something interactive. Discuss their views on drugs in sport, or the twin tower atrocity, or religious fundamentalism. There's enough to talk about at the moment.'

'Maybe you should let them select the topics,' Kate responded. 'You'll be surprised with what they come up with.'

Slowly she made her way to his office. Her mind churned, trying to puzzle out the problem. *Had something happened to her parents? An accident? A burglary at home?* There was nothing else obvious she could think of.

The two policemen introduced themselves and showed their identification badges. Both were in plain clothes; the older of the two appeared to be the spokesman.

'Can I confirm that you are Catherine Pritchard of 28 Manor Crescent, Oxford?' he asked.

'Yes, I am,' she replied. 'But everyone calls me Kate. Can you please tell me what this is all about?'

Namibia 1987

The sand was damp and cold; overhead the sky still clear, the sea-mist not yet in across the land.

He made sure that the camouflage groundsheet covered him completely. The balaclava was pulled well down over his face and neck. He continued to watch and wait. Like a burrowing animal he hollowed deeper into the sand, his senses alert to any unusual sounds or movements.

Up and down his eyes followed the fence line. To his left it stretched between him and the sea. And, as he knew, it continued for some two hundred kilometres further along the length of the security area.

The view through the night-vision binoculars was good enough as long as the mist held off.

Tonight would be the last — the last big haul and then he would disappear. Pay those that needed to be paid, then slip into South Africa and on to a flight overseas.

The crates were already packed and in Cape Town ready for shipping to Southampton. Tonight's haul would be hidden in the last crate still to be sealed. If everything worked out as he planned, a new financially sound and wealthy life awaited him. The thought sustained him as he hunkered down and remained ready.

It was so quiet. Even the raw Atlantic Ocean sounded like soft distant breathing.

As he lay there the usual doubts raised their heads. Maybe their modus operandi had been discovered. Or someone inside the security area had given the game away. But he had made five big hauls so far, all without failure. Everyone involved had received a share.

There was a quick movement to his right. *What the heck was that?*

Not wanting to take his eyes off the fence line, he reluctantly swung the binoculars towards the movement that he had picked up.

A scurry, and then he saw it. *A jackal!* Silently he breathed out. His focus shifted back to his priority area.

The dampness was increasing, the mist moving inexorably off the sea.

Maybe another hour, then visibility will be gone. I may have to abort.

He stretched slowly, easing his cramped joints. At least his feet weren't too cold.

Then, in the near distance, he saw a dark shadow change position. It moved slowly, crouched low to the ground.

The shadow moved in halting stages towards the fence. A few metres. Stop. A few metres. Stop. A few more metres.

He watched intently, training the binoculars on the shadow and adjusting the sights a little finer. His mind and body sank into a deep stillness, a technique learnt in military reconnaissance training all those years ago. In the poor light it seemed like an exaggerated movement as the shadow stood. There was a motion, the quick flurry of an arm throwing an object. The man saw something land on his side of the fence.

The shadow on the far side bent down again and painstakingly, crablike, made its way back in the direction from whence it had come.

The man remained totally still. The spot where the package had landed was indelibly fixed in his mind.

An hour passed. Slowly the mist descended and became thicker. With visibility down to less than ten metres, he made his move. Extricating himself from beneath the canvas cover, he slowly slithered forward. His clothes blended with the desert ground. In that dark, dank night with almost zero visibility, he knew that nobody could see him even if there was a patrol out in the vicinity.

The package lay exactly where he had marked it. He felt it carefully. It was very similar to the five previous ones - a thick wrapping of newspaper bound tightly with rough sisal string.

He tucked it securely into a uniquely fashioned inner pouch in his jacket.

Cautiously and very slowly he inched away from the drop-site. He crawled a bit then scanned the immediate area. Crawled further. Scanned. He knew the direction in which to go.

The mist was now a complete screen. He could hardly see anything. And, like some invisible wraith, he stayed undetected.

England 2002

'Miss Pritchard, we apologise for disturbing you at work.' The policeman seemed sympathetic. 'This will only take a few minutes.'

'Has something happened to my parents?' Kate asked worriedly.

He shook his head. 'No, not at all. We are making informal enquiries about Mr Pieter du Toit; very informal at this stage. We hope you will be able to help us.'

'Who? Mr du Toit? I am certain I do not know anyone of that name. Is he related to one of my pupils?'

'No, Miss Pritchard. We believe you do know him.'

'No...o, I don't think so.' She was clearly puzzled.

'You know him as Peter Dutton.'

'Peter? Has something happened to him? Oh, my God!' She suddenly felt deeply anxious. A band tightened around her chest. 'But his name - something doesn't make sense. You have it wrong.'

'Miss Pritchard, as far as we are aware nothing has happened to him. And the name is correct. When did you last see him?'

The policeman looked at her gravely.

'This morning before I came to work. We live together and have done so for more than two years.'

'Yes, we know.' The policeman examined his notes. 'We have a colleague arriving from South Africa later today. He would like to interview you if possible. Can we arrange to see you both tomorrow morning? Say...at nine o'clock?'

Kate looked doubtful, 'I'll have to ask Peter...'

'We could get a warrant,' the officer went on. 'But as I said, these are only informal enquiries at this stage.'

'It's Saturday and we're not working,' Kate said. 'I usually like to go to the gym early for a spinning class.' She tried to assert herself. 'Nine thirty would be better. Detective Randall, can you tell me what this is all about?'

He shook his head. 'I'm afraid I can't. Our South African counterpart will explain everything tomorrow.'

After they had left she sat for a few minutes trying to gather her thoughts. *What was going on? And why did they call Peter by a different name?*

'I think I need to go home,' she said to the head.

'Of course. Is there any way we can help you?' His concern was obvious. 'Shall I get someone to take you?'

'No, I'll be fine. It's all very vague. Something to do with my boyfriend.'

Before she drove off she tried to phone Peter. His number didn't ring at all; did not even go to voice message. The number appeared to be dead. When she got home she tried again. Still completely silent.

'Tea,' she thought. 'That's what I need.'

The note was attached to the kettle.

'*Under your pillow,*' was all it said.

She opened the letter first.

My Darling,

These last two years with you have been wonderful.

I love you so very much.

To leave you now is heart-wrenching and difficult.

Let my gift bring you happy memories of the two of us together.

My darling, as soon as you read this letter I want you to phone Andrew Rathbone. These are his telephone numbers 01865 412344 and 07595 285591.

You do not know him, but please contact him immediately. He knows who you are.

I understand that this is all very difficult. I hope that one day you will allow me to make it up to you.

With all my love
Peter

Her heart thudding, she unwrapped the gift box.

The stone glowed a vibrant sunset orange-pink - a cabochon-cut sapphire pendant in an exquisite gold setting. She turned it over. Their intertwined names were finely engraved on the back.

The beauty of the piece brought her to tears.

'Oh no, Peter, oh no,' she whimpered.

Slowly she tried to compose herself, but when she read his letter again the tears came back. Somehow his words indicated finality. An abrupt and unchangeable ending.

Taking a deep breath, numbed by what was unfolding, she dialled the first number.

'Mr Rathbone has just popped out for a few minutes. Can I get him to return your call?' a woman asked.

'I have his mobile number too,' Kate said.

'Good, try him on that. If you can't get hold of him just ring me back.'

The phone was answered on the first ring. 'I have been expecting your call, Miss Pritchard.'

'Peter...' her voice caught. 'Peter said I should contact you urgently.'

'Yes. Can you come and see me?'

'Today?'

'Yes, please. You are only ten minutes away.'

'What?'

'Miss Pritchard, my offices are in Summertown. You are just around the corner.'

'Mr Rathbone, you seem to know quite a bit about me,' she commented a little sharply.

'Yes, I do. But it's all in your best interest, of that I can assure you.'

***

The brass-plated sign outside the offices read:

> **ANDREW RATHBONE**
> **ASSOCIATES**
> **SECURITY CONSULTANTS**

The first thing she noticed about him was that he had the same military bearing as Peter. Straight-backed, confident, well groomed. And, like Peter, he looked fit and strong. His accent was similar as well - tonally slightly flat, typically South African.

A solitary file lay on the desk in front of him.

'Tea or coffee?' he offered. 'Oh, and please call me AR, everyone does.'

'Just a glass of water, please. My day appears to have gone from bad to worse.'

'To some extent I agree,' AR said smoothly. 'But at least I am here to assist you.'

'I am not sure I understand. The sign on your door...'

'Yes, it could be misleading.' He shrugged his shoulders and smiled disarmingly. 'Nevertheless, let us move on.' He opened the file. 'There are a few documents here for you to sign.'

'Mr Rathbone,' she interrupted, 'who are you?'

'AR, please. May I call you Kate?'

'Yes, of course.'

'Well Kate, I act on Peter's instructions.' He smiled again. 'Maybe we can do the paperwork first, and then I'll tell you what I can. I may not be able to answer all your questions, but you should get a better understanding of the situation.'

'Where is Peter?'

'Please, Kate,' his voice a little gentler, 'can we do this first?'

'Okay,' she responded dubiously.

'Good.' He handed over the first document. 'Could you please sign here, where I have fixed the little Post-It flags.'

Kate studied the paperwork. 'What is this? Something to do with the mortgage on my property?'

'Yes, your mortgage has now been paid up, including the charges and all related costs.'

'What? I don't understand?'

'Kate,' he said softly, 'Peter has paid off your mortgage. Your home is now totally your own.'

Her mind whirled. *Where had Peter found the money?*

'Mr Rathbone...AR,' she muttered hesitantly, 'I can't sign this. How do I know it's all legal?'

'You can sign it, I assure you. The funds are fully accounted for, all in the UK. It's perfectly legal.'

With a slightly shaky hand Kate signed the document where he had marked it. AR took it away and laid the next one in front of her.

'This is an insurance document increasing the value of your household contents. Please sign it as well.'

Kate took in the value. 'Ten million pounds! For my few things?'

AR remained nonchalantly silent.

'The contents of a small two-bedroom house - furniture, ornaments, fridge, washing machine, a few paintings and carvings - ten million?' She was incredulous.

'Peter has already paid the premiums for the next three years,' AR continued. 'This is really just a formality.'

'Mr Rathbone, are you playing games with me?'

'Not at all.' His voice was firm now. 'The necklace that Peter left for you - the sapphire. It's probably in your handbag right now. Please take it out and put it on the table.'

A little chastened, she did as she was told. 'How did you know about..?'

'How much do you think this is worth?' He picked up the piece and held it to the light.

'I don't know,' she replied hesitantly. 'Maybe somewhere between three and five thousand pounds.'

His grin was infectious. 'Multiply the three by thirty.'

'What?' she calculated quickly. 'Ninety thousand? It can't be!'

'Yes, Kate, it is. Ninety-five thousand pounds to be exact. It's a rare Padparadscha stone that comes from the Kashmir.'

Stunned, she sat back in the chair.

He flourished the last document. 'Please also sign this as marked.'

'What is this for?'

'This is an agreement between my company and you. How shall I explain it?' His fingers steepled under his chin. 'Simply put, you retain me to help you as and when you require help. If a car dealer turns you over. Or a builder lets you down. Maybe an insurance claim. Or your passport gets stolen in a foreign country. That type of thing.'

'All...'

He answered for her. 'Yes, my services are all paid for by Peter.'

For a moment there was quiet. Kate took a sip of water.

'AR,' she asked quietly, 'where did Peter get all this money?'

'That, my dear, I cannot tell you exactly. In fact, I can honestly say that I don't really know all the details.'

'But is he wealthy? Or...or has he just won the lottery?'

'Oh, he's very wealthy. Far greater than a lottery pay-out.'

'Can you give me an estimate?'

'Cash alone, excluding fixed assets, it's probably more than five hundred,' he replied mischievously.

'I'm not sure I understand...five hundred what?'

'Five hundred million pounds. Probably more. Maybe even a lot more.'

'My God!' The figure took her breath away.

'Yes. Peter has made a lot of money over the last ten to fifteen years.'

'How?'

Rathbone raised his hands. 'What little I know I cannot disclose. What I don't know is, at best, pure speculation,' he went on, 'but I am sure we will know more tomorrow.'

Kate said nothing; she was waiting for the next surprise.

'The police have made an appointment to see you?'

'How do you know that?'

Ignoring her question, his face betrayed nothing as he spoke. 'I will be there too.' He tapped the retainer document she had signed.

Kate drew in a deep breath and gathered her thoughts. *AR seems to be in no hurry. Well of course not, Peter's paying his fees!*

'How long...how long have you known Peter?' she asked haltingly.

Now it was his turn to look reflective. 'Let's see. I'm sixty-five and Peter is nearly fifty. He must have been eighteen or nineteen when I was his commanding officer, so I've known him at least thirty years.'

'You were in the army then?'

'Yes, we both served.'

'The South African army?'

'Yes, Special Forces Reconnaissance. We were called recces.'

'Where?'

'Mainly on foot in Angola and Zambia. Later on elsewhere - the Congo, Cabinda, Sierra Leone and so forth.'

'The South African army was in the Congo?' She sounded incredulous.

'No. Things changed,' he said offhandedly.

'So you became mercenaries?'

'More like private armies. We were employed by mining companies, engineering firms, even other governments.'

'Other governments?'

'Yes - the British, the Belgians, the Americans. All in vicious, difficult little conflicts.'

'So that's how you and Peter made so much money?'

'Kate, I wish I had, believe me,' he said. 'Peter has many hundreds of millions more than me!'

She looked around the spotlessly clean, spartan office. There were no photographs or personal things, no trinkets or adornments, only a painting on each wall. They reminded her of the ones at home.

'Can I ask two...no, three more questions? I hope you will be totally honest with me.'

AR looked at her and nodded.

'The connection between Peter and yourself - there's something more, I can sense it.'

His eyes seemed to change focus as he responded, the memory deep yet still vivid.

'Yes, there is. He saved my life. In Cabinda. I had been badly wounded and Peter came back for me when others had left me to die.'

'And so?'

'I owe him my life,' he said simply. 'And I would trust him with it.'

Kate let the answer settle.

Before she could speak again, Rathbone said quietly, 'And that is why you must believe in him too. I think I know what you want to ask next.'

'Peter…' her throat felt tight, emotion threatening to overtake her. 'Does Peter really love me? Or was I just some sort of…a fling, a passing fad?'

'Oh, Kate, that is so easy to answer. As you know, he is a kind, deep-thinking man. He absolutely adores you and will do anything for you. He is hurting deeply, but…'

'But?'

His words were circumspect. 'The situation does not permit him to be in the UK at present.'

'Will…will I ever see him again?'

'That I cannot answer definitively, but I think it could happen. If you are prepared to wait, maybe…'

'Mr Rathbone, what choice do I have? What choice has Peter left me?' Now she was openly sobbing, shuddering from deep within herself. 'He is part of me. I am one person made of two halves - he and I. He is my life.'

**

All night she tossed and turned, continually reaching out to where he normally lay. His clean, subtle aroma was still present on the sheets and pillows. As she lay there, trying not to cry anymore, she wondered how one coped with tragic bereavement. When one's partner suddenly died after years of being together, or when a precious child was lost.

She felt bereft. It was deep and cutting; a pain worse than anything she had ever felt before.

Just after six in the morning she walked through the door to the Health Club. There was hardly anyone around. She climbed onto an exercise bicycle and pedalled until her legs were screaming. Then she attacked the weights' rack and trained until her arms and shoulders were in a similar state of exhaustion.

'I will deal with this,' she muttered to herself over and over. 'And I will find Peter. I'll get that smug Rathbone to help me.'

By the time she got home she felt better. While waiting for the policemen to arrive she spent some time on her computer scrolling through articles on Cabinda, the Congo and Sierra

Leone. She read of confrontations and skirmishes she had never considered before.

There were reports on organisations like Executive Outcomes and other similar set-ups. Even ex-Prime Minister Thatcher's opportunistic son was involved in dodgy arms deals with rebel groups.

South African mercenaries always seemed to be involved. Diamonds almost always seemed to be the bounty.

She also had a brief look at articles on the South African Special Forces, and there she found two names that warranted a second look. Colonel Linford and Captain Rathbone. The two men had developed an elite reconnaissance unit that was later called 31 Battalion. She scanned the information quickly. Words like 'unorthodox', 'operate independently', 'guerrilla tactics' and 'irregular warfare' jumped out at her. At least Rathbone had an identity to her now.

It was a world far removed from her own. *I'll follow this up some more later. I need to understand these men.*

Then she began searching for Peter's name elsewhere on the internet - through the Who's Who, the *Sunday Times* Rich List, wherever she could find links.

Nowhere did he appear.

***

Namibia 1987

He unbolted the heavy thick-tyred spare wheel from his Jeep Wrangler and laid it on the workshop table in his garage. Before he started he checked once again that the garage door was properly locked and the screen across the window firmly taped down. He rotated the spare wheel until the cuts in the tyre tread could be clearly seen. Using a sharp Stanley knife, he opened and lifted the flap he had made for the previous shipments.

One by one he fed the specimens into the long, slender, lead-lined compartment, counting as he did so. His eyes widened at the size of some of the stones, but this was not the time to admire.

He kept counting until he had finished. 'Eighty-six,' he murmured.

Carefully he closed the flap and re-sealed the cut-lines with vulcanised rubber. When the vulcanising had firmly set, he mounted the wheel back onto the roll bar bracket. He studied the mounting carefully. It would take an exceptional eye to see that the tyre had been tampered with.

He tidied up the toolbox and packed it next to his suitcase in the loading box.

Driving slowly through the back streets of Oranjemund, he made his way to the main exit gate. *Four years gone in a flash.*

'Mister Piet, you are leaving us today?' The security guard was a plump mixed-race man, sometimes a little careless, but always with a friendly demeanour.

'Yes, Bennie, I'm on my way. Time for a new start.'

'*Ja*, Mister Piet, that's what I keep saying to my missus, but she won't let me leave her for a new start,' he laughed. 'But what the fuck, I live a good life.'

'That's right, Bennie, your wife is far too good for you. And your children are very special.'

'*Ag*, Mister Piet, you have been a good boss to me. Let me just check your car, then you can be on your way. Maybe bring your case and toolbox into the office and we can check them as well.'

The search through his belongings was more thorough than expected. They took everything out of his suitcase and felt the inner lining carefully. His toiletries were scrutinised, and any container that could conceal contraband was closely examined.

Bennie and his colleague then packed everything back neatly.

'Sorry, Mister Piet,' his tone slightly abject, 'but we are just doing our jobs. As you taught us. Where are you headed for?'

'That's okay, Bennie. I'm going to take a few months off. Spend some time in the Okavango swamps, Vic Falls, you know, just travel around. Maybe Serengeti, that sort of thing.'

'Well you go safely, Mister Piet. Me, myself, I've never seen an elephant or a lion in the wild. What sort of African am I, heh?'

The guard offered his hand and they shook. Pieter du Toit started his Jeep and drove slowly through the security gates.

***

He breathed deeply. The most difficult part was done. He would be in Cape Town by nightfall; the next day he would meet with the shipping agent to finalise arrangements. The buyer for his car was waiting to take it over. Then he would catch the overnight flight to London and endure the six-week wait for the crates to arrive.

The roads were long and straight, the scenery spectacularly barren and desolate. When the rains came everything changed; then the glorious Namaqua daisies would be out in full flower.

He drove steadily, staying well within the speed limits. As he travelled he allowed his mind to wander. The next phase of his life was ahead and there was substantial planning to be done.

In Cape Town the following day, everything went like clockwork. One of the shipping agents' workers helped him seal the final crate. The six packages were carefully concealed in between his collection of semi-precious specimens, all tightly packed in newspaper and bubble wrap.

He signed the customs declaration forms and paid the shipping fees.

The agent came across. 'We'll load your crates into the container of another client of mine who is moving overseas. There's space at the back of it. The container is scheduled to arrive in Southampton in forty-three days.'

'Shall I phone you then?' Pieter asked.

'Not necessary. My office will contact you once it has customs clearance.'

'Shouldn't we have left the crates open for the local customs people to inspect?'

'No, man, they never check this stuff - hobby stuff like collecting silverware or books or ornaments. They couldn't give a damn.'

Collecting 634 illegal uncut diamonds is hardly a hobby, Piet thought wryly to himself.

England 2002

She had gone to the kitchen to make tea when something struck her; a connecting flash of memory that took her back to Andrew Rathbone's office.

'The paintings,' she breathed. 'And my insurance!'

She had never questioned the small pictures that Peter had hung in the hallway. There were two, both by the same artist. The name looked like *Cejar* but she wasn't quite sure.

At the top of the staircase was the other one he had brought home.

With the lighting and her soft furnishings, the paintings blended in well. If anything, they were slightly understated. At the time she had thought they were fine replicas. In fact, Peter may even have intimated that, led her to believe that he'd had them for some time.

But now? She did a quick search on the internet. The name she typed in did not appear, but there were suggested links to others.

'Where shall I look? I know nothing about art,' she muttered to herself. 'I'm just a Maths and Science teacher. Maybe Cezanne?' she typed it in.

The material on Cezanne was extensive. A catalogue of his work appeared and one of the images immediately caught her eye.

'Oh my goodness, look at that,' she spoke aloud. 'I'm sure there's one just like that in Rathbone's office.'

Reading quickly, she tried to find the other name. 'Pissarro. I think I've heard of him.' She was about to read more when she heard someone at the door.

England 1988

'Pieter, my boy, how are? Your recent telephone calls were most intriguing!' Solly Lichtmann was a large effusive man, slowly turning plump. 'It's been a while, Pieter. Let me see, Cabinda, what...eight years ago?'

'It's about that, Solly.'

'What you did there, Pieter, for me and my associates - we are forever in your debt. Let me give you a hug. Moira, come and meet Pieter du Toit.' He gestured the woman over.

She was nearly as large as Solly, with cold glittering eyes that matched the diamonds on display.

'I'm pleased to meet you, Mr du Toit. Solly has often spoken of you. He says you are a remarkable, resourceful man. I believe we may be doing some business together.'

Pieter lifted the haversack off his shoulder. 'Hello, Mrs Litchmann. I remember what Solly once told me - he's a hard negotiator, but he said that he's like mud when compared to you.'

'We try to make a modest living,' her smile did not quite extend beyond her lips.

Solly clapped his hands. 'Lock the shop and switch off the phones, Moira, let's see what's in that bag of Pieter's.'

Slowly they unpacked the six parcels, spreading the diamonds across a black velvet-covered table.

Solly's face showed his astonishment. 'Pieter, how many are here?'

'By my count 634.'

'*Oy vey!*'

There were twenty-two exceptionally large stones which Pieter kept apart from the rest.

'It will take us a while to value them all.' Solly fitted a loupe to his right eye and, with a fine pair of silver tweezers, began separating the stones. Moira did the same.

Pieter watched as they deftly examined and sorted the gems. Every so often one of them would draw an admiring breath at the beauty and quality of a particular stone. Halfway through they stopped for a break. Moira made tea and the three of them chatted as if what they were doing were some normal everyday occurrence.

'I think we can afford to give lunch a miss; this is more important.' Solly grinned. 'We should probably give lunch a miss every day, Mrs Lichtmann.'

Steadily the diamonds were evaluated. Using a code known only to Solly and herself, Moira calculated and kept notes. Then they scrutinised the last twenty-two stones that Pieter had set aside.

'You know, Pieter, this may be too large a transaction. Even for me.'

Pieter's eyes were steadfastly serene. 'Solly, I have a proposal to deal with that.'

Even in the cool elegance of his Hatton Garden boutique the Jewish man was perspiring freely. His mind and thoughts were dominated by the size of the hoard, by the possibilities and opportunities it would bring.

He studied Moira's notes and figures. 'Come, let us sit over here and marvel at those rough beauties from a distance while we talk.'

He opened a cupboard, taking out a bottle and three fine-cut crystal glasses. 'A little forty-year-old malt will smooth the way.'

'So, Pieter, what do we do now?' He took a long, deep swallow.

'Solly, it's straightforward. You and Moira know what these are worth. And I know what they are worth.'

'But Pieter, these are illegal diamonds! Outside the system! And it's a very large haul!'

'And?'

'I normally get parcels of twenty or thirty through the Central Selling Organisation. Legally, and then perhaps only two or three times a year.'

He took another deep swig. 'Your hoard is six years' supply to me.'

'Solly, look down this street. These are all your friends. You all go to synagogue together, you socialise every Friday. If you wanted, you could share the sale with them.'

'Some of these bastards,' Solly said mock-seriously, 'all they really want to do is cut my throat!'

'But you get my point.'

'Yes, I could move a few around.'

For the first time in hours Moira spoke. 'Pieter, if we don't take them, what will you do?'

She had gone straight to the crux of the situation.

'I think that's why I know my proposal will work.'

'Wait.' Solly poured himself another drink. Moira and Pieter declined.

'I want thirty million for the 612 smaller diamonds,' Pieter said calmly.

'Thirty million, *meshuggah*!' Solly interjected. 'You are a crazy man, Pieter!'

'Solly, my dear,' Moira spoke soothingly. 'You'll give yourself an attack. We haven't heard the rest of Pieter's proposal yet.'

'The other twenty-two stones are where the big money is,' Pieter went on. 'And as you can see, when cut properly, they will each make two or three or maybe even four more jewels. They are yours for almost free.'

'What?' Now Moira spluttered. 'There...there must be a catch!'

'There is, but it's not very difficult to resolve. Not for you.'

'Pieter, what do you think the twenty-two are worth?'

'A million apiece and more.'

Moira and Solly exchanged glances.

'That's maybe a bit high,' Solly muttered. 'But...but there are some exceptional stones there.'

Nobody spoke.

'What must we resolve?' Moira asked softly.

'First, I want a British passport.'

'And?'

'I will require that you purchase paintings for me. Small masterpieces which I will identify from time to time.'

'Do I have it right - *for* you, not from you?'

'Yes, *for* me. The first six will cost you about half a million each. Any piece that costs above that, I will send you the additional money. Or make a financial arrangement to suit yourselves. Any further paintings that I ask you to obtain for me I will pay for in full.'

The Jewish couple looked amazed.

'So, what you want for these 634 diamonds is,' Solly gathered his thoughts, 'just so that I understand properly - thirty million in cash, three million towards art pieces, and a British passport.'

'The paintings - that is what binds us. Some sort of informal, unwritten contract?' Moira clearly understood the proposal. 'We are your agents. You are invisible.'

'Yes, you could say that. The art may take a few years to resolve, for the right pieces to be found.'

'But,' Moira asked, 'how are we going to arrange the thirty million? Do you have an account in Switzerland? Or somewhere offshore? The Cayman Islands?'

'It's getting more difficult these days,' Solly stated. 'There are much stricter bank disclosures and exchange controls.'

'No,' Pieter grinned mischievously. 'That is the easy part.'

'Really?'

'Yes.' He looked at them confidently, knowing that the deal was done.

'Come on, Pieter, don't string us along!'

'I want it paid or, should I say, made available, in Israel.'

England 2002

The doorbell rang. When Kate opened the door AR stood there with Detective Randall from the day before. Alongside them was a third man, thickset and solid, his face ruddily sunburnt.

Kate ushered them in. She saw the big man glance at the paintings hanging in the hallway. His eyes gave nothing away.

The third man and AR clearly knew one another. There was an ease between them indicating they might even be friends.

'Don't tell me you two also served together!' Kate was determined to be on the front foot; the session in the gym had fuelled her indignation and intensity.

AR smiled ruefully. 'Kate, this is Captain Prinsloo of the South African Police. Japie Prinsloo. I have known him for a long time.'

'And?'

'I was his commanding officer too.'

The British policeman looked on; he said nothing but was clearly curious.

'So, Captain Prinsloo, you were also a recce. Like Peter. In all probability you know him.' Kate took a breath, and then spoke again. 'Is someone prepared to tell me what this is all about?'

'Yes, ma'am. I will.' The big South African's face relaxed into a genial smile.

The mood in the room immediately lifted.

'Thank you very much for agreeing to see me; I know this is not easy. You are obviously bewildered and confused.' His voice was heavily accented. His manner, on the surface at least, appeared informal and considerate. 'Ma'am, you are correct.

Pieter, or Peter as you know him, and I served under Colonel Rathbone.'

'Were you also a mercenary?'

AR looked surprised at her sharply directed question.

'No, ma'am. When I finished military service I joined the South African Police and have been working there ever since.'

'So, what do you want from me?'

'Ma'am, I know it may be difficult, but I would like you to help me. And help my British colleague here as well.'

'And why would I do that?'

'Because ma'am, and I am really sorry to be the one to tell you this, because my government and the UK authorities have agreed to Pieter's extradition back to South Africa...'

'Japie,' AR interrupted, 'that is not strictly correct. There is an agreement in principle only at this stage.'

'*Ja*, Colonel.' Even after all the intervening years there was a great deal of respect in his voice. 'You are right. But we, my government, we are confident that the paperwork will be finalised shortly.'

Kate made to speak, but AR held up his hand. 'Wait, Kate, maybe it would be better to end this meeting now. Let's wait until we know all the details first.'

'But there are things I want to know now!' Kate knew she sounded petulant, but somehow Peter's story needed to be told; she needed to know what was going on. She was hurting deeply, emotionally; the wrenching ache inside her craved to be appeased. Only more knowledge would do that.

Japie looked at AR. 'Colonel, let me put the cards on the table. It is only fair to Miss Pritchard. Let the lawyers handle the legal stuff.'

AR took his time before responding. 'Okay, Japie, but I will decide if there are any questions to be answered. And how far we go with this.'

'That is fine, Colonel. No problem.' He looked down at his hands and then up at Kate. 'Ma'am, Pieter is one of those exceptional men. He grew up street smart and tough, becoming even tougher as he got older.'

'What do you mean by that?' Kate asked.

'At the end of Pieter's military service, he joined - in most cases led - mercenary groups in various parts of Africa.'

'Mr Rathbone has already told me about that,' she said.

'Yes, but did he tell you all of it?'

'What do you mean?'

'Ma'am, these were hellish places. Violent, corrupt, remote. If something went wrong there was often no way out.'

'And so?'

'What I am trying to say is that Pieter was the best. Everything he had learnt in the South African army, everything he had learnt from the Colonel here, and from others, he applied.'

'In what way?' Kate was intrigued.

'Careful planning, meticulous preparation, rehearsals. His selection of men - hardened and highly trained. The best weapons and equipment to suit the circumstances.'

'He left nothing to chance is what you are trying to say.'

'Precisely, ma'am. And all with one aim.'

'Which was?'

'Diamonds, ma'am. He only ever got involved when there were diamonds.'

'Diamonds?' She spoke aloud.

'Yes, ma'am. He would take some payment in cash, but the remainder he always took in diamonds.'

'Do you mean...what's the term?' she tilted her head. 'Red diamonds? No, that's not it...blood diamonds?'

'Yes, ma'am, something like that.'

'But AR, you must know something about this?' Kate glared at him accusingly.

Rathbone shrugged his shoulders. 'There was always some talk. There always is. But I was seldom involved.'

'Are you telling me that Peter traded in illegal diamonds?' Now she stared angrily at the South African policeman.

'Yes, ma'am. And more. Let me tell you what happened in Namibia about fourteen years ago.'

His narrative was enthralling.

He told Kate that along the diamond-rich shores north of Oranjemund, the beaches are stripped to bedrock by the mining company. The sand overburden is removed for processing through screening plants where the diamonds are separated.

Back at the exposed bedrock, the cleaning teams move in. Every crevice and fissure is scoured and cleaned. The residual diamonds are then collected for sorting and processing.

'But what has this got to do with Peter?' Kate asked.

'He was Chief of Security at Oranjemund for just over four years,' the big policeman replied. 'He was employed based on excellent references, including one from Colonel Rathbone!'

'And so?'

'During the second half of his employment term there were six significant dips in production. Dips out of the norm.'

'Come on Japie,' AR interrupted. 'That could be easily explained.'

'Maybe.'

'Sure. Poor weather, mechanical problems, labour unrest, Christmas holidays. Any number of things.'

'Still maybe. But let me tell you a little more.' Prinsloo's grin was infectious.

'About two years ago, the Namibian authorities discovered a smuggling network which worked something like this.' He took out his notebook. 'I think it will be easier if I make a sketch.'

In a surprisingly artistic hand, he drew the sketch.

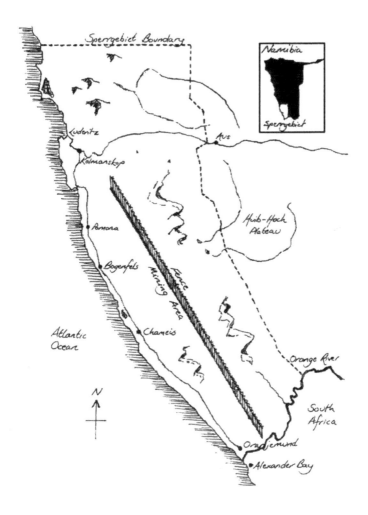

'This is the Sperrgebiet, in other words the security area. And this is the mining zone along the coast. Within it are numerous mining areas. It's all fenced along here. What happens is that packages of rough diamonds, hoarded by the bedrock cleaning teams, get thrown over the fence. Somebody waits on the other side to collect them.'

111

'So, the person waiting is in open country?' Kate asked. Without knowing why, the question sounded naïve.

'No,' Prinsloo replied. 'This area is also secure. And patrolled. And it is desert - vast and inhospitable.'

'So how does someone get the diamonds out?'

'People have tried all sorts of methods - microlight aircraft, small helicopters, light planes, overland on motorcycles. Most, almost all, attempts are unsuccessful.'

'Japie,' AR interrupted again. 'I think you need to bring this to a head.'

'Okay, Colonel, I've got the message.' He looked around the room. 'We believe that we have enough evidence against Pieter du Toit to arrest and extradite him. But it would be much easier if he came back to South Africa and Namibia voluntarily to answer the charges.'

'Come on, Japie, what you have told us is just a long story. Where's the proof, man?'

The big policeman appeared unperturbed. 'Colonel, the evidence is strong. One: we have broken the smuggling ring. We know which workers in the mining area were involved. Two: their families and chiefs who illegally benefitted are known. Some are already in custody. Three: Pieter has been named as one of the conduits in the time that he was working there.'

'The conduit?' Kate asked. 'What does that mean?'

'He was the cash conduit. We think he somehow retrieved the diamonds. We know he sent the agreed cash north to those benefitting.'

'You're sure?'

'Yes, ma'am. We have witnesses and their statements.'

'This all happened years ago,' AR said. 'Sounds like you're trying to find a scapegoat.'

The policeman shook his head. 'No, I don't think so. Point four: as I said before, during Pieter's years in Oranjemund there were six significant dips in production. We still have the records.'

'Japie, that proves nothing. We've already discussed this,' AR's voice remained calm and controlled.

'Colonel, Pieter left Oranjemund and went to South Africa each month following the dips. Six times. We have records for those too.'

Kate's stomach felt hollow. The man was confident and assured. She wondered what would happen next.

AR took over. 'Japie, we can't help you. Miss Pritchard knows nothing of this.'

'Nothing?'

'Absolutely. Up until yesterday she believed that Pieter worked in the city doing banking security.'

'You mean to tell me that Miss Pritchard knew nothing of his wealth? His contacts in Israel? His contacts with the Jews in Hatton Garden? And all the rest?'

'Absolutely. She knows nothing.'

'Miss Pritchard, what did you two talk about?' The policeman sounded doubtful. 'Look at the million-pound paintings on your walls - small magnificent masterpieces!'

'I don't think they're originals,' Kate said in a small voice.

'Come on, Miss Pritchard,' now his voice was coldly sceptical. 'One of them is by Cezanne. Even a dumb Afrikaner like me can see what they are!'

'Japie, we'll end this now,' Rathbone said firmly. 'Whatever it is you want from Pieter you'll have to find him yourself.'

'I will. I have been tracking him for many years.' Japie Prinsloo grinned and stood. 'As in the old days, I'll keep going, Colonel. You know I will.'

***

'Where is Peter now?'

AR sat at the kitchen table while she made coffee.

'Kate, I can't tell you.'

'Is he safe?' Kate felt drained and empty; her hands shook as she poured.

'Oh, yes.'

She sighed and dropped her head into her hands. 'What…will happen now?'

'Nothing. Japie Prinsloo is a good policeman, but Pieter is light years ahead of him.'

113

'And me? Do I just go on as if nothing has happened? Peter and I are in love - is that also just nothing?'

'No, Kate. You carry on bravely. You live in hope. You let me help you.' He studied her carefully. 'And I will. And Pieter will, too.'

'But?'

He gave her a small smile. 'You will have to be patient.'

'For how long?' she wailed.

'There is no answer to that.'

***

Zambia 2003

She stood in the queue waiting for her visa to be scrutinised and her passport stamped.

The customs officer checked her through. Fifteen minutes later she walked into the arrivals hall and looked around. A small plump man with a welcoming smile held a handwritten board with her name on it.

'My name is Rojabu, but only my mother calls me that. Sometimes my boss also does when he is cross with me,' he said with a grin. 'Everybody else calls me Roja. Or behind my back, that useless bloody Roja!'

Katie couldn't help but laugh. 'And I am Kate Pritchard.' She held out her hand. He took it in a light, soft, deferential grip.

'I am your driver and guide, Miss Kate, from now on until the end of your trip.'

'The lodge where I am staying has arranged this?' she questioned. 'This personal service? I thought there would be other guests too?'

'Miss Kate, today you are the only one.'

At the back of the room a man lingered behind a column, bush hat pulled well down on his head. He would shave off the beard later.

As soon as he saw her he knew the right decision had been made. She was tall and slender and ever so lovely; a lissom, blonde beauty.

The yearning of the last ten months began dissipating as he looked on.

'Just a little while longer; another two days maybe,' he said to himself. 'What is that after all this time?'

'Roja, how far do we have to drive?' she asked.

'Today we drive five hours. To my village where I was born. We stay there tonight; tomorrow we go on to the lodge.'

'And how far is that?'

'The road is not good. Maybe three, four hours.' He smiled. 'I always make the journey in two sections, otherwise too much for my guests and myself.'

Kate grinned inwardly. *His guests.* Did he know the budget that AR had given her? Even though she hadn't paid for anything yet other than her flight, the wad of cash in her money belt was inordinately thick.

She thought back to her discussion with AR. 'I want to go on holiday.'

'Where do you want to go?' he had asked.

'You white Africans have completely turned my life upside down, so that is where I want to go. To Africa, where I've never been before.'

'Whereabouts in Africa?'

'I don't know. Somewhere really remote. Where there are elephants. Where the lions roar. Back to the damn bush - that's what you lot always go on about!'

Outwardly she purposely made herself sound acerbic, but inwardly she rather liked AR. He was suave and dapper, and always treated her with dignity and as a valued friend. Always stayed in touch.

'There is a place I know - a small, very exclusive lodge. Let me speak to them and I'll get back to you. Does half term in October suit you? During the school holidays?'

'Yes, that's fine. And where is this place exactly?'

'In Zambia. Deep in the Kafue Reserve.'

'Zambia? I was thinking of South Africa or Botswana. Something like that!'

'Trust me, this place is special. Let me see what I can arrange.'

The rondawel was neatly built and painted light blue. It had a thatched roof but no windows, just fixed flyscreens in the openings. The building was cool and clean and functional. White linen and a bright orange batik covered the bed.

Roja's sister, who looked and smiled just like him, brought Kate one bucket of hot water and another of cold.

'For washing you,' she said simply.

Kate's dinner that night consisted of small pieces of grilled chicken served with rice and a salad of tomato and onion circles. The simplicity of the meal; the village children sitting wide-eyed and endearing around her, sometimes asking shy innocent questions; the wood smoke of the cooking fires - these would form a memory that surfaced often in her life ahead.

The next morning they drove on. The road was washed away in many places and potholes - sometimes a metre deep - had to be avoided and circumvented. There was no traffic, just an occasional motorcyclist or intrepid locals on old-fashioned black bicycles.

They were seeing more wildlife now - impala that gazed at them placidly, and a group of young kudus that ran across the road.

It seemed to Kate that the road was gradually tapering, as if coming to an end.

Eventually Roja slowed right down. Pointing, he said, 'We turn down here along this track. Then one more hour and we will be there. No rain these last few weeks, so we can get through quite quickly.'

'There are no signs. Or anything,' Kate mused. 'I hope you know where you are going.'

'Don't you worry, miss,' Roja responded, 'my place is very special.'

His assertion of ownership amused her once again.

They kept on going, wending their way down to a large river. The expanse of the water surprised her; it had to be at least three hundred metres wide.

'We park here, Miss Kate. Under this tree.'

'Are we going to cross the river?'

'Yes, miss, this is the Kafue River. My lodge is on the other side. Listen!' He cupped his hand to his ear. 'They hear us driving through bush, now they come to fetch us.'

'Whose place is this?' Kate queried.

Roja paused before responding. 'My chief, he and another man own it. Plus the workers. We all have a share.'

Kate's curiosity was pricked. 'The other owner, who is he?'

'Big businessman, miss.'

'From Zambia?'

'Yes, miss.'

'And his name is?'

Before he could answer, a speedboat pulled onto the shore. Excited greetings were exchanged. Kate's bags were loaded, plus boxes of provisions that Roja had clearly shopped for prior to her arrival.

'Come miss, you sit here. We go across. The boatman is Albert.' Solemnly the man shook her hand.

Kate sensed something remained unspoken.

She sat and looked around as they motored steadily across the river. She found it difficult to take it all in; the landscape was wild and primeval, untamed, no impression made by man on it.

Roja touched her arm. 'Look, miss, hippo. Over there, see the pink ears? And there, back on bank.'

'Are those...crocodiles?'

'Yes, miss, big ones here. You must never go near the river alone. They will easily take you.'

The lodge was like some exotic Eden she had always imagined but never thought could exist. The buildings were set low, the green roofs below the line of the indigenous miombo woodland. Along the hewn stone walls the neatly cut lawns were green and lush. In the humid warmth the flowers and plants grew profusely; Kate noticed a gardener was on his knees thinning out clivia almost as tall as himself.

The lady who met her was big and robustly attractive. She made no attempt to shake Kate's offered hand; instead she wrapped her arms around her in a broad embrace.

'Miss Kate, we have been waiting for you. For a long time. Welcome, welcome!'

'This is my wife, Princess,' Roja intervened. 'Let's show Miss Kate to her room.'

'Let me look first at this beautiful woman. Instead of looking at an ugly old man like you.' Princess's spoken English was pitched and diction perfect, reflective of expensive foreign schooling.

'How…how many guests do you have at the moment?' Kate asked.

'There is another couple, but they are flying out tomorrow. Then for the next week you are the only one.'

My goodness, what is this holiday going to cost me? Aloud Kate asked. 'Flying? From where?'

'From here. They have their own helicopter,' came the reply.

***

The dining room opened onto the gardens. Sounds that she did not know filtered in - birds, insects, animals; it was all wonderfully different. The other couple turned out to be a handsome silver-haired man she guessed was close to sixty and his companion, a dark olive-skinned beauty probably half his age. They kept to themselves and spoke in a language that Kate did not recognise. At times it sounded like Russian or Polish but then, for some unknown reason, she thought it could be Yiddish.

That night she slept better than she had in months. She slept like she used to do with Peter next to her - secure and calm and at peace with herself.

A gentle tapping on the door woke her.

'Good morning, missie. I am Lucas,' he said when she answered the door. 'I bring your coffee. When you are ready, I bring your breakfast. Specially made for you.'

A table had been set under a graceful whitethorn acacia. Again, as on the previous evening, the setting was immaculate; gleaming silverware and Stuart crystal glassware adorned the table. The breakfast was her favourite: a light fluffy omelette served with finely cut cheese and tomato. The bread was white, and still warm from the oven.

Kate sat there and ate quietly, indulging in the sights and sounds of the bush. A sudden crackling in the bushes alarmed her - the sound of branches being broken.

'Elephant,' Lucas said. 'Going down to the river to drink. Later I, or Roja, will show you.'

'Where do you come from, Lucas?' Kate asked.

'Missie, I come from south. Near Namibia border.'

'That is far away. How did you get to be working here?'

'Well...' Lucas hesitated before responding. 'Well, missie, Princess is my daughter number four,' he said proudly. 'She has the brains of all the others, boys included.'

'How many children do you have?'

'Eleven, miss.'

'My goodness, that is a lot!'

'Yes, miss. Six boys, five girls.' He smiled. 'A mixed football team,'

'And Princess? Why do you say she is so clever?'

'She went to university, miss. The first in my family. And in my wife's family. The only one of my children.'

'And she went to university here in Zambia?'

'No, miss. She went overseas.'

'Really. And if I may ask, where did she go to?'

'To Cambridge, miss.'

'Cambridge...in England?' Kate knew she sounded incredulous.

Lucas grinned. 'Yes, miss, Corpus Christi College.'

'My goodness. What degree did she do? What did she major in?' Kate wondered what the next surprise would be.

'She did quite good.' Lucas could not disguise the pride in his voice, but at the same time, he appeared to become a little reticent. All the same, he went on. 'First she did a degree in Mathematics. Then she did a Masters in Chemical Engineering. She has a doctorate now.'

'Quite good? Lucas, that is amazing.' *How did an African woman from a small, isolated rural community achieve this?*

'She's been to America too, miss.'

'What? Don't tell me she has an MBA as well?'

'Yes, miss. From Boston Harvard, miss.'

Kate's mind spun. Princess had to be one of the most highly educated women she had ever met. And yet, incongruously, she lived out here in this incredibly wild remote area.

119

How this all connected was beyond Kate. There seemed to be a thought, though, a spark, like a low flickering candle, which flared briefly in her mind before dying down.

'But, Lucas,' she couldn't help herself. 'Where did you get the money for all her education? It costs thousands - hundreds of thousands - to get an education like that!'

He would not be drawn any further. 'Maybe tomorrow you will know more, but today you rest. I show you swimming pool. There is gym for exercise. If you want massage or manicure or your hair done - my daughter number three is ready. I will arrange. And later,' he pointed in the direction of the river, 'I will walk with you to see the elephants.'

She did as Lucas suggested and the day seemed to glide by.

At four o'clock Lucas and Roja were at her door. Kate was surprised to see that they were now both dressed in military fatigues, each with a large calibre rifle slung over their shoulders.

It made an immediate impact on her. The bearing and attitude of the two men had undergone a distinct change; these were well-trained soldiers accompanying her.

They walked steadily in a wide loop through the bush. Every so often the men would stop and point something out to her. At one spot a velvet-black bateleur with its bright red cere gazed down at them from the top of a high mahogany tree. Closer to the river a group of handsome waterbuck allowed them to approach before slowly drifting deeper into the bush.

Lucas squatted down in the dusty path. 'Look, Miss Kate,' his fingers traced the outline of a paw print. 'Lion. Big Lion. Still fresh. Maybe crossed here less than an hour ago. Look - here front feet, one, two. Here back feet, one, two. We must keep our eyes very open.'

A few minutes later he held up his hand. Standing close to Kate he murmured, 'Can you smell?'

'Yes.' The odour was rank and pungent.

'Look. Can you see?'

'Yes. Elephant. Aren't we too close?' Her voice trembled as she whispered back.

'No, it's okay. We will watch from here,' Lucas replied.

'The smell,' Kate said, 'it's very strong.'

'Yes. The bull is rutting. In musth. That is why we should not go closer. It can quickly become dangerous.'

Once the sun dropped below the height of the trees Lucas quickly led the way back to the lodge. By the time they arrived the lights were already on and glowing in the various buildings.

When Kate sat down to dinner that evening, she felt she was glowing and replete. Everything was totally different, her senses overloaded with new experiences. But still her mind toyed with random thoughts. She tried to connect them mentally; nothing really made sense.

There is only one way. The school teacher in her took over. *Write them down; make a list.*

She took a note book and pen from her bag. As she ate her dinner, and with Lucas in attendance from time to time, she tried to formulate her thoughts into some sort of order.

1. Rathbone suggested Zambia. Why?

2. Nobody will tell me who the owners are. By design or not?

3. Look at this place. The luxury. The attention to detail. It could almost be somebody's home. Very large home. Is it?

4. Princess - education. Where did the money come from?

5. Princess - what is her role? Said they had been waiting for me. For a long time.

6. Lucas, Roja - were they soldiers/mercenaries?

7. People yesterday; own helicopter - Israeli perhaps?

8. The food - how do they know my favourite dishes?

Realisation hit her almost instantaneously. The shock brought an involuntary gasp as her hand went to her mouth. 'Peter. This all belongs to Peter. It must be. Oh my God!'

She sat there, stunned. 'He's the thread that ties this together.' Her words were loud and tremulous, reverberating around the room. A tremor rippled through her. Shoulders dropping, she could feel herself shaking, sinking and then weeping.

Lucas said something. It sounded like, 'Stay here, I come back now.' But the words didn't really penetrate. All she could now feel was the dam-burst of emotion flooding within her; the loneliness of the last months, the longing, the heartache and sadness.

There were footsteps behind her but she did not look up. Her head remained buried in her arms. Her sobbing shook her body in deep racking convulsions.

Somebody placed their hands on her shoulders. She knew the touch.

He spoke gently. 'I have missed you so much.'

***

Pieter du Toit came from the rough and ready southern suburbs of Johannesburg; he was partly supported by a bullying, anti-social father whose wife had left him a week after Pieter was born. His mother had been raped into a baby she neither wanted nor cared for. If the baby had been a girl, she would have ended its life before fleeing. A back-street abortion had been out of the question, the cost unaffordable and, in those days, the danger to her health enormous.

Pieter's father was a railway official of unknown authority, but was apparently well paid.

From the age of five the boy had been sent to boarding school, a life he would lead until he left school just before his seventeenth birthday. Placing him in a good school was the only decent thing his absentee father ever did for him. His parting words: *'Let somebody else worry about you while you are getting a good education,'* still resonated all these years later.

Pieter grew up in the school hostel. Even during holidays he remained there. The stern Afrikaner matron kept him fed and made sure that he washed and ironed his clothes.

Military conscription followed. Midway through his first year of service he attended a recruitment briefing for a new reconnaissance unit being established in the Western Caprivi - South West Africa. There Pieter found his niche. Small operations were where he thrived as a member of two or three-man tactical teams, operating deep in foreign territory. These were situations where one had to remain calm and contained under pressure. Situations where lifelong loyalty to your fellow comrades was born.

Leon Kaplan became his closest friend. A tough little Jew, his grandparents of Polish descent, he was intelligent and sharp with an inborn ability and aptitude to repair anything mechanical or electronic.

The two men became inseparable.

'In 1976 when Leon and I completed our military service, he moved to Israel. I became a mercenary. I was working for high stakes, but the risks were high too,' Peter said. 'And there were always diamonds involved.'

Kate took his hand. 'But, Peter, it was illegal. Even immoral. How could you reconcile yourself to it?'

He was unapologetic. 'I realised a long time ago that the only way I could really change my life was to get money. To make some sort of real contribution to the society I wanted to live in, and find the place where I wanted to live, I had to have money. Lots of it!'

'But, Peter…'

'My darling, try to see it from my side. Look at my upbringing, my military training. I had no higher education, no parental guidance. I had to make use of what I knew best. I had to find a way.'

Underneath her eight-point list, he made a list of his own, sketching out the size of his financial holdings. 'So, this is what it looks like now:'

DUTTON HOLDINGS	USD 400 million
DUTTON INVESTMENTS	USD 200 million
KAPCO ARMS	USD 400 million
DUTTON / KAPLAN PROPERTIES	USD 150 million
OTHER SMALLER CONTRACTING AND MANUFACTURING COMPANIES	USD 200 million

'But how did your wealth escalate to these sorts of figures?' she asked tentatively.

'Leon Kaplan started an armaments business…'

'Making and selling guns! You make money trading in illegal weapons too?'

'No, Kate,' Peter shook his head. 'Hear me out. Leon began working on missile guiding packages, designing very precise bombing systems. The forerunner of the drone industry - unmanned weaponry, cyber weaponry.'

'And?'

'He and I were partners. Are partners. From day one.'

'And?'

'I provided the initial financial stake. Leon, and the small team he built around him, did the design and development.'

'In Israel?'

'Yes, it's an Israeli business.'

Kate was quiet for a moment as she digested what Peter had told her.

'If I understand it properly, and from what I have seen on TV and read in the newspapers, then your systems are being used by the USA and by the UK. I think I mean NATO. And who knows by who else. And where...in Syria and Afghanistan and Yemen and Iraq and Turkey and South Sudan and...'

'Yes, my darling,' Peter said quietly. 'They have bought our systems.'

'For vast amounts of money.'

'Yes.'

'My God! And now you are worth over one billion dollars?'

'Yes,' he smiled gently. 'That's the conservative figure.'

'Conservative?'

'That's my nett worth. The gross is nearly double that. There is ongoing work, ongoing development, deals being structured all the time.'

'But you live here in the bush? In this most remote of places.'

'Yes, but Princess doesn't.'

'Princess? How does she fit into all of this?'

They had been sitting and talking for hours. Peter called out softly and Lucas came padding in. Peter said something to him in a language that sounded like Dutch or Flemish. Kate later learnt that it was Afrikaans.

The black man returned a few minutes later carrying a tray with tea, coffee and biscuits. He placed a decanter of golden-hued white port on the table as well.

'Lucas never seems to sleep,' Kate remarked as she watched Peter pour the coffee.

She was tired and it was late, but now something else was taking over. It was an inner happiness bubbling up; it was the joy of being with Peter again. She loved his assured confidence. He looked fitter than ever and was clearly still in love with her.

'It's because I'm back and you're here,' Peter responded. 'He looks over and after me.'

'What do you mean because I'm here?'

'Because he knows that you are the person I love.'

'You mean his loyalty to you extends to me?'

'It's more than that. It's because of what you mean to me. His loyalty, his duty, is to protect you, look after you. For me.'

'Peter, that is so intrinsically deep,' Kate whispered. She could feel tears coursing down her cheeks. 'Why would he do that?'

'You remember the three-man teams I was telling you about, from my military days?'

'You mean that you, Leon and Lucas were a team? There were black soldiers in the South African Defence Force? In those days? During apartheid?'

'Oh, yes. There were many reasons that they, and the Angolans and the Bushmen, joined the SADF, but all were integral to our operations,' Peter asserted. 'Our team was exceptionally well trained and exceptionally successful.'

'So that is why the bond is so strong between all of you. Even Japie Prinsloo seems to belong. His respect for Andrew Rathbone is immense,' Kate said.

Peter nodded. 'Japie is a good man. He was a fine solder, too. And, from what I have heard, he is one of the best police officers in South Africa.'

'Doesn't it worry you?'

'Worry me?'

'That he's trying to arrest you!'

'No, my darling, his resources are far too limited. And...' Peter chose his words carefully, 'we always know what he is up to.'

Kate wanted to ask him what he meant, but then she remembered her earlier question and that took preference. 'Princess; tell me about her. Her educational achievements are quite astonishing.'

'Many years ago Lucas hauled me out of a very difficult situation. But that's a story for another day.'

'I won't let you forget,' Kate murmured.

'I promised Lucas then that I would help educate his children. It was what he wanted above all else. It was a pledge that I kept.'

'So you paid for her education.'

'Oh, yes, and for some of the other children too.'

'But she is different.'

'Yes. She has a remarkable brain and is a workaholic. Studies and knows every detail.'

'And she does what in your business exactly?' Kate asked.

'She does the deals,' Peter replied simply.

'The deals? What do you mean?'

'She negotiates the sales of our systems; is in charge of those deals. She and the team that she has built up are exceptional.'

'My goodness, she's the one who makes the money!'

'I wouldn't quite say it like that, but yes, she's a skilled negotiator. Princess knows the technicalities of our packages inside out and has a vast array of contacts in the defence departments of many different countries.'

'How has she managed to do that?' Kate asked.

'She earns respect. By her work ethic, her integrity and her honesty. And, like many Africans, she's a linguist too - speaks a host of languages. Obviously English, but also French, German and Spanish, with a good working knowledge of a few more, including Arabic.

'What about Chinese, Mandarin?'

'No, we will not deal with the Chinese. It's a fundamental decision.'

'Why not?'

'Because once they have a product, they copy it. They reproduce the technology, ignoring the patents and legal rights. In the end you have no market left.'

'And yet, despite all her accomplishments, Princess is married to Roja. How does that work?'

Peter thought for a moment before responding. 'I've also wondered about that over the years. They have no children, which is extremely unusual for an African couple.'

'They can't have children?'

'Correct. The problem lies with Princess. She is also a little older than Roja. So...'

'She spoils and mothers him instead.' Kate giggled at the remark, remembering the soldierly Roja who had accompanied her to look for elephants.

'Yes. She adores him but they also spend a lot of time apart.'

'She lives in Tel Aviv?'

'A black woman in Israel? That wouldn't work!'

'Why not?'

'My darling, the Israelis are dreadful racists. No, she and her team are based in London. We have offices there.'

'Where you used to go when you were living with me?'

'Yes, sometimes. I also had an office at AR's place.'

'That damn AR! He always knew more than he was telling me.' And then another lightbulb clicked on. 'He works for you, too.'

Peter looked down and then up again. Looked at her directly. 'Yes, my darling, he works for us. Head of Security.'

'So that's your executive team then - Leon Kaplan, Princess, AR and yourself.'

'And our Chief Financial Officer, Hyman Cohen.'

'The man who was here yesterday. With his own helicopter?' Kate asked.

'Yes. The helicopter...'

She didn't let him finish. 'Is yours!'

Peter grinned, leaned across and kissed her softly.

Zambia 2010

Peter Dutton runs his business empire from electronically sophisticated offices deep within the African bush. The offices are powered by a vast bank of solar panels and batteries; there is a huge backup generator and two large satellite dishes are carefully sited.

Surrounding the complex lengths of railway track have been concreted deep into the ground as fence posts. The fencing is heavy steel cabling strung between the posts; it is the only way to keep out inquisitive elephants.

That evening when he laid his hands on Kate's weeping shoulders, she had made him tell her his life story in detail. Some things she already knew of, but he did not try to hide anything from her.

The full extent of his wealth is known only to himself and two others - his wife Kate and a silver-haired Israeli accountant based in Tel Aviv. At first the enormity of his holdings was beyond his new wife's comprehension, but over the years she has become an integral part of its ever-increasing growth and management.

Kate has an uncanny judgement for sound, principled investments; she is the moral compass that guides their future.

MAGIC FLOWER

Zambia / Zimbabwe 2012–2017

The elephants had been restless all the previous night.

As the sun rose, the clamour continued. They were more than restless and unsettled; they crashed and rampaged through the surrounding bush. Branches could be heard breaking - limbs torn from trees, bushes uprooted. The commotion resounded across the vast Zambezi River Valley.

The elephants seemed to be dangerously alarmed. Something had seriously disturbed them. From where we camped, it sounded like they were in anguish.

All day we stayed close to our base, carefully quiet and out of their way. Even Elijah, the camp guard, remained in his hut.

It was blisteringly hot and oppressive. At midday the temperature was 43°C with humidity levels in excess of 85%.

But this did not deter the elephants. Normally still and quiet in such heat, they ignored the shade. They remained troubled and anxious. There was no pattern to their restlessness; groups would go down to the river and quickly drink, then move off frantically into the bush again.

My wife, Karen, and Elijah and I, were the only people in the immediate area. The nearest village was forty kilometres away. When we met the local game ranger there a few days earlier, he told us that poaching had been all but eradicated. In fact, the men of the village who had previously, in the main, been the poachers, were now effective and aggressive gamekeepers.

Human presence was clearly not the reason the elephants were now so upset. Something else had made them distraught.

The setting sun projected a blushed orange radiance over the width of the river. We watched as small flocks of green-glossed ibis flew past, making their way to roost in the remote swampy areas upriver. The elephants appeared to have moved on.

I was busy dismantling my camera and tripod when the boats came past, outboard motors discordant and at full throttle. It was the fleet of speedboats from the exclusive tourist lodges downstream.

There were calls to our camp guard and he shouted back. It was all unusual, unclear and confusing.

I asked him what it was all about, the dangers of travelling on the river at night obvious.

'I do not know, *bwana*,' Elijah replied. 'They say they go to fetch someone or something. But I cannot hear properly.'

An hour later the small armada returned. Two of the speedboats veered towards us. The second boat lay low in the water, its engine strained and misfiring. By the light of our campfire and torches we could see the people in it bailing furiously. To sink in the Zambezi, with the ever-present danger of crocodiles and hippos, was a peril to be avoided at all costs.

We helped to haul the stricken boat up on to the riverbank. From below the gunwale came a muted low squealing and a powerful stench of animal faeces and fear.

A baby elephant lay there, legs bound and tied down. Its breathing was tortured, seemingly restricted. One eye was visible, red-rimmed and terrified. The little creature could only have been a few days old.

My wife wanted to reach out and console it, but I gently held her back. 'I don't think it's wise,' I said.

'What are you doing?' I asked pointedly to one of the white men bailing out the boat.

He peered up at me. 'We have an enclosed camp at Mushika. We're taking it there.'

'What for?'

'To look after it, of course. Try and help it survive.'

'Where did you find it?' I asked. My tone sounded sharp. My wife glanced at me as I spoke.

'About five kilometres away. Abandoned. Lying under a tree,' he replied.

'Maybe…' I tried to choose my words tactfully. 'Maybe you should have left it there.'

Now the man looked surprised. 'That's not what we do here,' he replied aggressively.

'Maybe it was abandoned for a reason,' I went on.

'What?'

'Maybe its mother and the other females purposely left it.'

'What on earth are you talking about?'

I turned away, not wanting to provoke further argument. Karen took my hand and we walked back to our campsite. She knew what I was thinking.

Elijah came to join us, squatting down on his haunches, hands held out to the ebbing fire.

'You think the elephants knew what they were doing?' Karen asked me.

'Yes. Think about it; the elephants could easily have found it. Their senses are so acute and five kilometres is nothing.'

'I think you're right,' she mused. 'Perhaps something went wrong with the birth. Or it's damaged in some way.'

The black man nodded in agreement. 'Maybe head broken,' he said sadly.

Years later their words would resonate.

***

I lay there, eyes closed, but not sleeping. My body was in that state of fatigue where, after ten days of difficult hiking, meagre rations and carefully measured drinking water, all it wanted was to recover. Not to move, not to climb, not to perspire. And my mind was the same. All it wanted was to rest - not to concentrate on every step, not to be careful of every loose rock, not worry about standing on a somnolent puff adder.

The shelter of the shallow cave gave me respite from the blistering heat as it had done for others before. On the walls were finely drawn figurines, probably a few thousand years old. Lines of men and women, hunters and gatherers, accurately shaped giraffes and antelope.

I thought I might be the first white man to evidence the ancient rock art in that place. It gave me a feeling of deep awe and privilege. A naturally protected place, it was a small temple in the vastness of the Mavuradonha Mountains. Hiking through the remoteness and isolation had now brought me here - ever nearer to the first little villages and settlements.

I opened my eyes and looked down the escarpment to the northeast. At the limits of my vision a faint line of water reflected in the high midday sunlight.

Must be the Zambezi, near Cabora. Mozambique is probably only fifty kilometres away. No wonder there are no animals.

In the open spaces high up in the mountains and down along the watercourses there had been a few signs - occasional elephant and buffalo spoor - but my guide and I had yet to see anything.

Isaac had shown me why. Wire noosed traps rigged between bushes and trees, bullet casings at the waterholes, concealed spiked traps in the softer, sandier game paths. Even the birds seemed to be scarce and skittish, but maybe that was just my imagination.

In poverty-stricken Zimbabwe poaching was rife.

***

'Boss, *bwana*, please come quickly!'

'Why?' I sat up, shaken out of my reverie.

'Please, you must come.' My guide, a wizened man, not as old as he looked, was hand-wringing and agitated. 'There is accident, *bwana*.' His anxiety was infectious.

'What is it, Isaac? I'm really tired.'

'Boss, you must come. I will help you now.'

As I packed my kit and laced my boots, Isaac damped the small fire I had started and covered the ashes with a few rocks.

There seemed to be no point in trying to stop him; it was clear that he was determined to take me to the problem. When he'd slung my rucksack over his shoulders, he gestured for me to follow. Isaac might have been older than me and time-worn, but he could walk at a pace that I could barely maintain even when I was rested and fresh.

Up the track we went and across a rocky plateau. Twenty minutes later we forded a small stream. A water leguaan splashed noisily into the water directly in front of us.

'Nobody eats a bloody leguaan,' I muttered caustically to myself. 'They at least are safe.'

We hit a more well-used path and turned into it. I surmised that it was one of those typically ubiquitous tracks that connects every rural African village.

Waiting at a junction were two women. One took my kit off Isaac and put it on her head, the other indicated that we should follow her.

We moved higher up the mountain at a brisk pace - over boulder outcrops and through scraggly bushes which snagged at my clothes.

Sweating profusely, I had to stop. I drank a little water and offered the bottle to the others, but they all shook their heads. My pedometer indicated that we had already travelled nearly four kilometres from my short-lived camp. In that heat, and always going uphill, it seemed so much further.

We moved on, now a little slower. The woman guiding us called out and there was an answering shout. She swung left. Every so often I could see elephant tracks. Sometimes they were clearly defined, other times not evident at all or obscured by people's footprints.

Soon there was another shout and a small group of women and girls came into view. They were standing in the shade of a large acacia tree. Something lay on the ground before them. They had rigged a blanket over it to provide further cover from the sun, and one of the younger women had a leafy stem which she waved back and forth as a fly whisk.

A rucksack, torn open, had been thrown into the bush. Pale blue garments which appeared feminine in nature were strewn around. Nearby was a smashed water bottle. What looked like a tripod lay bent and broken in the sand, and alongside it a camera in smithereens.

I squatted under the blanket and took a closer look.

A white woman lay there unconscious, her breathing very shallow. She appeared to be in her sixties - deeply sunburnt, with long tangled grey hair strewn with leaves and dirt.

'Elephant, boss,' Isaac murmured.

'I wonder why?'

'Bad elephant, boss. We know this one. Bad from child. Bad till now. It moves like Tokoloshe.'

'How old is it?' As I slowly examined the woman I saw her mouth was choked with blood and what looked like bits of bones. They were broken teeth.

'Still young elephant, maybe five, maybe six years. Stays alone, boss.'

My eyes moved downwards. The woman's right lower leg was angled almost ninety degrees to the knee. Carefully I lifted the trouser leg. Her knee was smashed to a bloody pulp.

I couldn't see any other injuries, but there was the possibility of internal damage or a broken pelvis. Her trousers were soaked in urine; at least I hoped it was urine and not some evidence of deeper organ injury.

'Whew!' I whispered. 'What now?'

'You can help her, boss?' Isaac asked worriedly.

'I am not a doctor,' I replied. My tiredness made me edgy. 'Where is the nearest hospital?'

'It is far, boss. Very far.' I looked at him impatiently.

Isaac shrugged his shoulders. 'Maybe forty. Maybe fifty kilometres away. I not sure.'

'The nearest clinic?'

'In my village there is place.'

'How far?'

'Not so far. Maybe five, maybe ten kilometres.'

I drew a deep breath. 'How long will it take us if we carry her?'

'I think in three hours we can make it.'

'Telephone?'

Now he was more positive. 'There is sometimes cell phone reception near my village.'

I looked at the badly hurt woman and gathered my thoughts.

'We'll have to carry her down. Can you make a stretcher?' I sketched in the sand as I spoke. 'Two poles. And splints each about so long. And we'll need some rope.'

The group around me looked uncertain.

'Then we will have to move her on to the blanket and lift her in. Like this.' I gestured with my hands.

'No rope, boss.'

'Something else maybe - vines or strips of bark or thick grass that we can plait. You know what I mean. Like how you tie the thatch onto your roofs.'

Isaac turned and spoke. Two of the women moved off towards a small stand of white-berry bushes; one had a machete in her hand. Isaac walked the other way, probably to relieve himself.

While they were all busy I cut a strip off my shirt and wet it with a little water. My water bottle felt dangerously empty and I was sweating heavily in the high afternoon heat.

I'll need water soon. Especially with what lies ahead.

One of the older girls crouched down to help me. Gently she held the damaged woman's head as I carefully opened her mouth and cleaned it. As best as I could, I scraped out the broken teeth and debris. Using a small stick wrapped in a shred of damp cloth, I cleaned the congealed blood from within her nostrils.

She seemed to breathe more freely after that and her eyelids fluttered briefly.

The girl next to me knelt lower and spoke softly into the woman's ear. The Shona words sounded soothing and comforting.

It took nearly an hour before we were ready to move her.

We made the stretcher to fit snugly so that she could not roll around. I tested the plaited grass-rope, even tried to break it. The group just grinned at my futility.

Then I cut away the woman's trouser leg and exposed her broken leg. There was a collective gasp from those around me. I knew I had to straighten it so that the woman could lie properly on the stretcher.

The girl bent to help me again and I told her what we had to do. Firmly she held the woman's shoulders down. Holding the smashed knee in my left hand, I gently pulled the tibia into line and tied two splints down the length of the leg.

The woman groaned and heaved. The pain must have been excruciating, but at least she seemed to be regaining consciousness. Carefully we wrapped her in the blanket from my kit and lifted her onto the improvised stretcher. We tied more rope over her in cross-straps. She now lay securely in place.

***

The journey back along the tracks took four hours. Going downhill was hard; occasionally one of us would stumble or fall.

I was struggling. I tried to ration my water to small sips every fifteen minutes. When I offered my bottle to the others they always declined; they could clearly see that I was overheating and drained.

The girl who had helped me earlier was carrying the left corner directly in front of me. Every few hundred metres she would turn and smile. She seemed to be worried about me, seemed to be trying to support me in some way. As if through her encouragement I would be distracted from the immense fatigue that I was feeling.

It appeared to be working, but I found there was more to it.

The distraction was the girl herself. She was quite tall for her age, with a lithe easy gait. I thought she could be fourteen or a little older, but it was difficult to judge. Maturity comes early to African women.

In all aspects she was totally different to the other villagers with me. Her skin was lighter - pale brown - hair straight and black-sheened and with a slight wave into her neck. Her face too was finer featured, not as fleshy and rounded as the local people.

I watched her as we laboured on, mulling over her origins in my mind. It helped to detract from the distress my body was going through.

I thought about the rogue elephant too. Somehow the incident that Karen and I had experienced in 2012 surfaced. *Was there some connection? Could it be the same elephant?*

Slowly we made our way down. Every so often the woman on the stretcher would moan or cry out. Her eyes were more focussed now and she seemed to understand when one of us reassured her. She tried to say something, but the words were distorted and unintelligible.

We arrived in the village just as my legs were giving way. Black spots floated across my eyes and I had a terrible headache. We lowered the stretcher in the shade of a small structure and I sank down, almost fainting.

The guide shouted. Within minutes there was a large plastic bowl filled with tepid muddy water in front of me. Resisting the urge to drink, I bathed my head and the back of my neck.

I took my T-shirt off and soaked it in the bowl, then put it straight back on. There was a gathering breeze; I could feel my body-heat slowly reducing.

Isaac hovered worriedly over me. 'Boss, are you okay?'

'My rucksack; I'll need it. There is another bottle with some water in it, and some pills.'

'I'll bring it, boss.'

'And the clinic, where is it?'

'It's this building, boss. The key is coming.'

The building was decrepit and run down. A faded Red Cross sign hung lopsided on the door. All the window panes were smashed. Rusty corrugated iron roof sheeting clattered loosely in the wind.

There was a soft touch on my shoulder. The girl stood there. She had a key in one hand and a large enamel mug in the other.

'Drink.'

The red-bush tea was lukewarm and very sweet.

'Drink,' she said again. 'Very slow.'

As I drank, she unlocked the steel door. It screeched as she opened it. The building clearly hadn't been used in years.

I stood, swaying, and breathed deeply. Started to feel better as the headache slowly diminished.

'I bring more tea,' the girl said, and took the empty mug from me.

'What is your name?' I asked.

'My name is Mashiripiti Ruva. It means Magic Flower.' Her smile was irrepressibly sweet. 'I back soon.'

A few minutes later Isaac arrived with my rucksack. An elderly man accompanied him.

'This is village chief, boss. He has come to help us.'

Together we lifted the stretcher and carried the injured woman inside.

The room may once have been a clinic, probably back in the colonial days, but now all that remained was an iron bedstead in one corner and an empty steel locker fixed to the back wall.

'Is there a nurse?' I asked.

The chief had a sonorous deep voice, his English perfectly pronounced. 'The white farmers built this clinic, sir. But when

Mr Mugabe gave the land back to us, the farmers left. And the nurses went with them,' he added.

'That's more than thirty years ago,' I said.

'Yes, sir.'

'What will we do with this poor woman now?'

Neither of the two men replied.

We lifted the stretcher and placed it on the bed. The woman whimpered as we lowered her on to the iron frame. *Maybe there was damage to her lower back or pelvis after all.*

'Can you phone?' I asked. 'For an ambulance?'

The chief was glum. 'Sir, I have no phone. We do not have land telephones anymore. The cables have all been stolen.'

'I meant cell phones.'

'I am sorry, sir,' the chief looked even more disconsolate. 'There is no reception in this area.'

I frowned at the two men, my frustration and tiredness close to the surface. 'We'll need to get this woman to a hospital - very soon. Look at her!'

'Yes, sir, we know. But what can we do?'

'I have a phone. Where is the nearest signal?'

The two men spoke between themselves. As the conversation went on, the only word I understood was 'motorbike'.

Isaac spoke next. 'In the next village from here,' he pointed towards the north, 'there is a man with a motorbike. We will send a message to him.'

'We can't put this woman on a bloody motorbike,' I exploded.

'No, boss, that's not what we mean,' he held up his arms appeasingly. 'We will get him to take you over the mountains. Down to Guruve. There is a police station there. Sometimes a doctor is there too. And the Catholic sisters have a hospital twenty-five kilometres further south.'

He looked at the chief who nodded affirmatively. 'There you will get help.'

I weighed up what he had said. There seemed to be no alternative.

The chief looked at me expectantly. It took a moment for the penny to drop. Literally.

'You need some money,' I stated.

'Yes, sir. The motorbike man will need money.'

***

Dusk was approaching, the western horizon ochre-red as the sun went down.

I was exhausted. Wearily I erected my tent and made a small fire, laid out a few rations and ate slowly. Out of the twilight Magic Flower joined me. She told me that the chief and Isaac had left to find the man with the motorcycle. We boiled water and filled my flask and water bottles. Then, with Magic Flower's help, I cleaned the woman on the stretcher. Very gently we wiped and bandaged her leg, fixing the splints which had skewed loose.

'Clean her. Very carefully,' I said, and pointed to the woman's soiled pelvic area.

I looked away as Magic Flower lowered the woman's trousers.

The girl asked for my knife.

'Why?' I asked.

'I will cut panties off. Very dirty. Then I can wash her better.'

While Magic Flower was busy I crushed and diluted six painkillers in some water. Together we managed to get the injured woman to swallow them.

We covered her with my thermal blanket and propped up her head to keep her airways open. I checked her mouth and nostrils again; her breathing sounded much better. The woman spoke, but I could not understand what she was saying. At least she was now fully conscious which seemed to me to be a good thing.

We left the door to the room open in case we were needed, and settled down to wait it out until the morning. Magic Flower would not hear of leaving me alone. 'We must be here for lady. To help her.'

The night was warm and humid as the earlier breeze had died down. It was far too hot to make use of the tent, so I stoked the fire and made myself comfortable in the sand next to it. The girl did the same on the opposite side.

My eyes were continually blinking shut, and eventually I slept - exhausted, but at least no longer dehydrated.

Whether it was the strange subliminal noise or the pressure on my shoulder I wasn't sure, but I awoke startled and disorientated. The fire had burnt out; just a few glowing orange coals remained.

During the night Magic Flower must have crept closer. The touch that had awoken me was that of her arm draped across me. I lay still and gathered myself, trying to identify the strange sounds that I could hear. The surrounding darkness and my mind seemed to be entwined, reluctant to be separated.

The injured woman was crying hoarsely. Guttural and pain-racked.

Magic Flower stirred. I disentangled myself and switched on my torch, and she smiled as the light played over her face.

'I hear,' she said. 'We go see.'

The woman was half sitting, half slumped, but fully conscious. The noise we had heard was her calling for help, the words eerie and distorted from her damaged face.

'Herrp, herrp, pleesh ...' Over and over.

I quickly moved across to the bed. Her splinted leg had slipped; gently Magic Flower and I placed it back on the bed. Desperately the woman grabbed at me, tried to speak.

'It's okay. We are here,' I reassured her.

I shone the beam along the length of her body. In the confined space of that small room the smell of faeces was very strong. I turned to the girl, but she had already gone. A few minutes later she was back.

'Let me do.' She held a bucket of water and a cloth. 'I do.'

Gently I helped calm the distressed woman who groaned as Magic Flower washed her again. Her pelvis had to be broken.

Taking small sips of water she managed to swallow three more painkillers. I dared not give her any more. We settled her again, drew the blanket around her body and tucked it tighter under the stretcher. She tried to speak; it sounded like, 'Thank you.'

'We are just outside the door,' I said. 'It will be daylight soon and then we'll go for help.' The woman nodded, sighed and closed her eyes.

***

Outdoors it was still dark although the sky seemed slightly less black to the east. Dawn was still more than two hours away.

Magic Flower produced a small wire brazier. She placed a few pieces of charcoal from the fire on it and blew over them steadily. The coals glowed a soft pink, slowly turning crimson. She blew a little harder and added a few more lumps.

We poured water from my flask into a battered lid-less kettle and waited for it to boil.

The scene was so simple and domestic. But my mind and thoughts were anything but serene - they were swirling in turmoil. I was unsure about the bond that seemed to be developing with this unaffected and unsophisticated girl-turning-woman. The bond I felt was conflicting with my overriding concern for the gravely hurt woman in the ramshackle building behind us. And then there were my own personal circumstances with all that had happened to me in the past year.

Magic Flower knelt and scooped some of the warm water into the bucket. She lowered the top of her wrap and washed her arms and upper body thoroughly.

In the glow of the small fire her developing body was beautiful beyond belief, lissom and strong, skin aureate and smooth. Without inhibition she let me watch her, her eyes trusting and solemn.

She finished with a small shiver, the air cooler now before first light. Drawing the wrap around her, she sat down beside me. From within its folds she produced an old-fashioned broken-toothed tortoiseshell comb. Her hair shone as she combed it through in straight, regular strokes.

I poured the red-bush tea and slowly we sipped it, sharing the mug until it was finished.

As if out of nowhere, from some faraway place, and with my mind sinking into the fire, the question came: 'You have wife?'

I shuddered, drew a deep breath before replying. The hurt within me was always close to the edge of my psyche.

'Yes...and no.'

Magic Flower looked puzzled. 'I no understand.'

My emotions whirled. And then I was speaking, telling this girl-woman, whom I had known for just a day, what I had not been able to talk of in seven months.

And as I spoke, something in me started to lift. Like a heavy mist burning off as the sun bombarded it. 'Karen. My wife. Died,' I said. 'Seven months and two days ago.'

Magic Flower gave a small sigh and shook her head sadly.

'She was having her lunch,' I went on. 'In a park. Sitting on a bench with her sandwiches and a book.'

'And?'

'She had started having these headaches...' I attempted to find the right words. 'One of them exploded.'

'She dead? Straight? No time to fix?'

'Yes.' The desperate image lay always in the forefront of my memory. 'They found her there. Slumped. Her book had fallen to the ground. A sandwich half eaten.'

'She old?'

'No,' and I trembled. 'She would have turned thirty-four this year. Five...five years younger than me.'

I told Magic Flower about her. About Karen's innate kindness and humility. How she would help anyone, no questions asked, no wish for gratitude or repayment. About her love of the outdoors, of Africa, and its people and wildlife. And more...of Karen's small idiosyncrasies, little things - how she always stirred her tea and coffee anti-clockwise, always ironed the dish towels and our underclothing, liked to talk to the birds in the garden.

Magic Flower listened intently. She leaned over and poured some more tea, handed it to me. Tenderly her fingers went to my face, touching the tears on my cheeks.

'There is more,' I muttered.

'You have children,' she said intuitively.

'Yes. A little boy. Three years old.'

'And he is where?'

'With his grandparents. My father and mother are looking after him.'

'They tell you to take holiday? To find...' she searched for the word. 'Peace?' Magic Flower's insight was way beyond her youth.

'Yes.'

Her hand moved into mine.

And as the blue starlings began their early morning chatter and squabbling, and as it became steadily lighter in the east, and as we sat there close together, something began to change in me. A regaining sense of steadiness, a slowly diminishing sense of inner pain.

***

The day passed in a blur of activity.

It began with a two-hour ride on the back of a motorcycle. The road was just a rugged car-width track. We sped on down to Guruve, slowing slightly over the rocky parts, then speeding up to forty or fifty kilometres an hour on the firmer sand. No helmets or goggles, only sunglasses to protect our eyes.

We stopped only once on the way. A huge mamba lay across the track, its body shimmering gunmetal grey in the bright sunlight. The snake reared angrily at our approach, black mouth gaping, dead eyes coldly assessing our intrusion.

It moved aggressively towards us.

The driver and I sat still. Almost frozen to the motorcycle. Not daring to move.

Deliberately and slowly withdrawing its challenge, the snake sank down and swung away from us. The distinctive forward–scaled rasp was clear as it moved off into the bush. Shaking, the terrified driver indicated that I should take over driving and he would sit at the back behind me.

The sergeant at the police station was reserved and slightly reticent, but not unhelpful. He listened as we explained the situation and then he spoke to the motorcycle driver.

'No doctor here,' the policeman said gruffly, 'but I will phone the church. You wait outside. Driver stay with me.'

Surprisingly the response took only ten minutes. The driver returned alone. 'The ambulance is coming. We wait here for it.'

'How long?' I asked.

'Maybe one hour.'

'And then?'

'It will follow us back to collect the lady.'

***

Cautiously we made our way back, the ambulance wending on behind us.

The word 'ambulance' was almost a misnomer. The vehicle was an old battered Land Rover with a few cabinets welded to the rear of the cab and a portable stretcher clipped into place. The vehicle had a fibreglass canopy over the loading box. Torn plastic curtains hung in the canopy windows.

But the ebullient driver and the two middle-aged nuns with him had clearly been trained. All the villagers watched as they smoothly and efficiently loaded the injured woman into the back and connected a drip into her arm. After a quick look at the type of painkillers I had given her, they selected two syringes and ampoules from one of the cabinets and administered the injections. Almost immediately these took effect and she fell asleep.

By three o'clock they were ready to leave. When I asked about payment, the younger of the two nuns, a serene woman of French origin, just said, 'The Lord always provides, but never quite enough. A little money for our fuel and medical supplies would be most welcome.'

I kept a little cash to see me through the next few days and gave all the rest to them. Given the circumstances, US$200 did not seem to be that much.

***

Other than when the ambulance had been present and the injured woman taken away, I had not seen Magic Flower all day. In the early evening she was still absent.

I kept to myself; I had to. My mind was full of emotions and disquiet. But one thing had definitely changed - talking about Karen's death had brought relief. Not closure, but a mental settlement. The torment I had carried these last months had affected everyone. I had imposed it on my parents, my work colleagues, my friends, and, young as he was, my little son.

Sitting there watching the flickering fire I knew that things would now get better. In just over two days' time I would be back in England with my boy, ready to face the future. One thing seemed very clear to me - in some form I would change my lifestyle. Maybe buy a new home, work a little less, possibly even change career. Start afresh to some degree.

And the girl-woman Magic Flower? Young as she was, did she feature in my future? That was more difficult to assess. I knew nothing of her but she had moved into my being. Could it just be the situation we had faced together, or was there something evolving, something deeper? Were my growing feelings for her based on loneliness and lust, or could she one day be my partner?

Doubts circulated too. Was she trying to attach herself to me in order to find a way out of the poverty and drudgery of her every day existence? Did she see me as an escape route, a path to a better life, education, prosperity? And then, once she was older and more established, would she leave me behind for someone younger?

The firelight weaved through my thoughts. Flaring and then receding. Flaring and receding.

It felt good to think about change. To look to the future. To feel desire again.

The physical exertions of the last two weeks. The chance incident with a woman trampled by an elephant. Meeting this beautiful mixed-race girl. After months of despair there were now tiny developing shoots of hope in my soul.

***

An unfamiliar noise, a rustle, woke me. I leaned up on my elbow and shone my torch around. The zip of my tent slowly lifted.

Magic Flower knelt there, her face revealed in the beam. Slowly she inched her way in, turned and pulled the zip down again. I made to say something, but she placed her hand over my mouth to silence me.

My thoughts were floundering. I had slept so deeply, mind and body slowly re-charging. I looked at my watch; it was one o'clock in the morning.

I made to get up, thinking to re-kindle the fire. But Magic Flower drew me down, whispering in my ear. 'It is okay. We are okay.'

Slowly I settled again. The temperature had changed and it was a little cooler. I opened my sleeping bag out wide and draped it over us. I did not know what to say or do. Who was to judge whether the two of us being together could be wrong.

And I was hesitant to ask her to leave. She had done so much to help.

My conscience eased, I lay there still and tried to relax. She turned towards me, eyes open and unflinching, a knowing confidence in them. She took my hand and held it. Neither of us spoke.

Incredibly, and despite the awareness between us, we must have slept. The lateness of the hour dominated.

When next I awoke she was curled up against me. Her hair, which she had washed in cheap carbolic soap, smelled fresh and enticing. My arms were around her, my right hand in the folds of her loose wrap. Softly I explored the contours of her body, fascination overcoming guilt. A young woman with slender pliable curves. She moved closer to me and turned slightly, buttocks pressing into my groin.

Almost involuntarily my hands moved over her breasts. They were small and firm, more rounded than expected; nipples tight and conical. I knew I had to stop. She seemed to sense it and thrust even closer.

My desire and lack of self-control was overwhelming. I could not stop. My hands roamed over her body and she moved sinuously in tune with them.

Suddenly something startled us and we moved apart.

The noise came again. A snuffling low moan. We could hear the kettle clatter, and what sounded like the brazier being tipped over.

'*Vusi*, I think,' Magic Flower said, her voice a little scared.

I half stood in the confining tent and pulled on my T-shirt. Magic Flower closed her wraparound and tightened the belt. She smiled uncertainly. 'I ready.'

The hyena glared at us, eyes glinting gold in the torchlight, kettle crunched in its huge jaws.

I shouted, but it just stood and stared at us without fear or concern. Magic Flower hid behind me. I picked up a rock from the fireplace and threw. It bounced once and, with a soft thud, hit the hyena on its rump. The animal's glare remained baleful, then with a snarl it turned and made off into the night.

'My kettle is gone forever,' Magic Flower said solemnly. 'Probably all the way to Mozambique.' And then she started giggling. Her laughter set me off too. For a few minutes we were both helpless.

I bent and stoked the fire and we sat down to watch it blaze. Soon the first sounds of the morning began. Although still dark and just before dawn, there were people up and about.

Isaac would join me soon. He had arranged for the motorcycle owner to take me to the bus stop in Guruve. There I would catch the first minibus to Harare.

'So,' Magic Flower said simply. 'Your wife is dead. But to you she is still alive.'

'Yes.'

'That is good.'

'What is good about a dead wife?' I asked, wryly macabre.

'Wherever she is, wherever her spirit flies, she will now know there is a new woman for you. Me, who will love and look after you. Me, who will become a new mother to your son.'

I stared at her. 'But you are only thirteen or fourteen. I am old enough to be your father.'

'I am much older,' she said assertively. 'But I have no papers to show you.'

'And your parents? What will they say?'

'I have no-one,' she answered dismissively. 'I was left here as a baby. I am just village slave.'

I studied her; her beauty was African and European in some exquisite mix. Guilt and turmoil swirled through me. She was so young. And yet in many ways so grown up. Rural girls in Africa develop very young in their hardworking demanding lives.

'You know I'm leaving, don't you? Flying to England tomorrow,' I said as I took her hand.

Magic Flower gripped it tightly in both of hers. 'Yes, I know. I understand. Your son needs you. He must not wait any longer. He is the most important. But...' Tears made her eyes glisten. 'But I am sure you will come back for me.'

'I cannot make any promises. My life is very different to yours.'

'You do not have to make promise,' she whispered. 'Please just come for me one day. Please.'

147

'But what if you find someone else? A younger man to fall in love with.'

'No,' she whispered. She stretched across and kissed me softly, hesitantly, 'I am one who will only love once. I know who I am. I already in love. With you.'

***

The email was headed: Greetings from Zimbabwe

Hello Evan

I'm writing to thank you for all you did for me back in April up in the Mavuradonha Mountains. The image of that elephant attacking me is still vivid and frightening.

I am very lucky to have survived; so fortunate that you and the local villagers were in the area to help me.

I can, of course, no longer walk. My photography days are over. The damage to my pelvis and legs will leave me in a wheelchair for the rest of my days. There is a small possibility that I may be able to use crutches to gain a little extra mobility, but this is definitely some time away. A knee replacement may help, but the cost for it to be done in South Africa is way beyond what I can afford.

You are probably wondering how I found your email address. Remember your business card? Well, soon after you left, Mashiripiti Ruva or Magic Flower as you know her, came to see me with it.

In fact, she moved into my hospital ward at the Catholic Hospital and has been at my side since then. She slept on the floor and spent all her time caring for me and also helping others in the ward. An unofficial unpaid nurse-aide and cleaner. It could only happen in Africa!

Now that I am home again and among my things, I have been able to help her in various ways. Magic Flower is still with me. I owe her so much.

I have now been able to get her documents in order. Luckily I know one of the consular officials at the Mozambique Embassy here. Between us we have managed to get a birth certificate and Mozambique passport for her.

As far as we can ascertain her full name is Lilliana da Costa Kero (Lilliana means lily-flower!) and she will turn sixteen in a few months' time. She may, in fact, be a little older. Her mother appears to have died giving birth to her; it is probable that someone would have registered her months later. Her father's details are unknown. He may well have been of European or Portuguese origin.

The flip side of her becoming a 'proper' citizen is that she is now on a holiday visa in Zimbabwe. She must leave here in sixty days' time and return to Mozambique.

This has obviously brought matters to a head.

A little reluctantly and against my better judgement (but then, who am I to judge), Magic Flower has persuaded me to write to you.
Magic Flower is very beautiful, mature and intelligent beyond her years, but her youth is ironically against her. She is totally committed to you, of that I am certain. However, the age difference between the two of you is so great.

If you want to live together, I hardly need tell you that in England, or in Europe, it will be very difficult. The authorities will not allow it. Prejudices and wrong perceptions will also make your lives intolerable.

I offer no solutions. I do not know you. All I can do is to try and assist in some small way.

I will give Magic Flower whatever message you want me to.

Obviously if you choose not to reply I will understand.

With all my gratitude,

Yours sincerely
Louise Ferreira

I read the email, and then again. Over and over during the next few days. The reply, when I sent it, was just a few words in a single paragraph.

***

'Is that where we are going to live, Daddy?' My son looked out the aeroplane window, his voice serious and at the same time slightly wondrous.

'Yes, down that way a bit. See those buildings?' I gestured. 'Just down from there.' The panorama was boundless all around us.

'Daddy, will Nana and Grandpa come and visit us?'

'Oh yes.'

'That's good. I want to show them.'

'Show them what?'

'The colours, Daddy, the colours!'

'Really?'

'Yes, Daddy, look!' The boy pointed. 'Everything is blue, white, green and blue. The sky is blue, the beach is white, the trees are green and the sea is blue!'

I could not speak; my love for him constricted my throat. His animation and excitement which had been on hold for so long were now releasing, almost fifteen months to the day after his mother had died.

We disembarked and made our way through customs. The wait for our baggage seemed to take forever. I looked around and saw somebody waving at us through the glass panels at the end of the hall.

It hit me then. The doubts I had harboured now cleared away in an instant by the certainty of my decision.

They were waiting for us at the doors - the elderly white lady in her wheelchair and, alongside, the girl-woman I had changed my life for.

Magic Flower bent down and hugged my son. She looked into his eyes and laughed tenderly, whispering something in his ear.

And for the first time in so long his smile was glowing and unrestrained.

THE LAST KINGS OF LUANGWA

Zambia 2018

The call came just after seven in the morning. Coffee cup in one hand, I answered the phone.

'Shaun, you must help me! Please Shaun!' Her voice sounded distant and very distressed. 'I don't know who to turn to. Don't know what to do!'

'Slow down, Beth. What's the matter?'

'Shaun, those barbarians killed Samson and Hercules!' she cried.

'What?'

'They murdered them. The bastards murdered them! Please Shaun, please come and help me.'

I could hear her crying softly, whimpering.

'Beth, where are you now?'

'I…I'm at the camp.'

'And where are Victor and Peter?'

'Victor had to go home. His father passed away last week. And Peter is sick. He's in bed with malaria.'

'And the girl? Where is she?'

There was a slight pause before she answered. 'Precious left two weeks ago. Said that she had to go to Mpika to meet a friend. But…but she's part of this problem.'

I tried to absorb what she was telling me. Her guard and driver was ill. The ranger was burying his father. Her young research assistant appeared to have gone missing.

'Shaun, are you still there?' she asked.

'Yes, Beth, I'm here,' I replied. 'Look, I'm in Lusaka now. Luckily I have a few days off, but it's still going to take all day to get to you. You know how far it is.'

I could hear her sharp intake of breath. 'Shaun, there's more - much more,' she gasped.

'What do…?'

She interrupted before I could finish my question, her voice now even more desperate. 'Can't you get here sooner? Get somebody to fly you up. Charter a plane. I'll meet you at the airstrip; I'll pay for everything.'

Beth paying for a charter flight! She was as poor as a church mouse. She gave whatever spare money she had to the women of the local community - paid for their medicines and their children's schoolbooks, helped with their clothes. She hardly had enough to fund her own conservation research or even to live off.

'What is much more?' I asked. 'I don't understand. This problem - what do you mean?'

'You'll see when you get here. I can't say anymore. I'm using the satellite phone and somebody may overhear.'

'Okay, Beth, sit tight. Let me see what I can arrange. How shall I let you know?'

'Oh, Shaun, thank you.' I could hear her relief. 'I'll phone you again in an hour. Thank you.'

The line went dead.

***

I sat there pondering who to turn to. Garth de Villiers seemed the obvious - probably the only - choice. I tried his number, hoping he was in town.

'Fucking hell, it's still midnight, man!'

'It's 7:15am. Wake up. And listen.'

'Fuck, you're grumpy this morning. What you need is a good shag. That will cheer you up.'

'Garth, just listen for once!'

'Okay, man,' he yawned loudly. 'I'm listening.'

'Beth called. She says Samson and Hercules have been killed.'

'Oh no, these fucking poachers!' Now he was wide awake. 'And this bloody government, the corrupt sons of bitches.'

'She wants me to help her,' I said. 'Fast. Go there - to her base camp.'

153

Garth didn't hesitate for a moment. 'No problem, man. I have a rich American couple to take to South Luangwa. You can come with us. I'll use Louis Rautenbach's plane; it's bigger and faster. We drop the Americans off then you and I go on to North Luangwa.'

'How soon?'

'I'll get hold of the Americans now; tell them the weather is changing. Or that we're forced to change planes. Some such bullshit,' he went on. 'Tell Beth we'll be there between eleven and twelve - maybe even earlier. In the meantime I'll get these Yanks off their arses.'

Garth de Villiers was one of those - an old-school bush pilot, foul-mouthed and wild. But beneath the reckless façade lay another persona, one that was caring and sincere, even at times rather gentle.

The American couple were clearly important. The US ambassador to Zambia had personally brought them to the hangar where the private plane stood waiting.

While Garth did his pre-flight checks I told them the real reason for the urgency. They were surprisingly understanding.

'We heard from a friend of ours this morning that poachers have killed two of the most important animals in the North Luangwa Park,' I said. 'She has asked that we go up and help her.'

'What was killed?' the man asked. In bearing and stature, he looked and sounded military. His wife stood next to him, clearly also someone used to authority - and used to being in authority.

'The largest male elephant and the only adult male black rhino,' I replied.

'And you know this for sure?'

'Yes,' I replied. 'Both animals were so important to that area that they wore GPS tracking collars. Our friend has been collecting data on them for the last three years.'

The American woman looked shocked. She was about to say something when Garth called out for us to board.

The noise of the plane's engines drowned out any further conversation until we were well into the air. Turning around to face me, the woman asked for more detail. 'You said those poor animals were very important. Why?'

'The black rhino was vital to the gene pool. As far as Beth, our friend, knows there are only nine other rhinos left in North Luangwa. Four are adult females, three juvenile females and two very young, and this is not certain, males.'

'And the elephant?'

'He was huge. Magnificent. Probably about thirty-five years old with a wonderful pair of tusks. He was quite a character.'

'In what way?'

'He liked to visit the base camp. Would stand just at the edge of the clearing, watching the activity. Sometimes Beth would leave a few oranges out for him or a loaf of bread.' I could feel emotion rising within me. 'Hercules just loved a treat. He always seemed to know when Beth had been to the village markets.'

'It's so sad,' the woman said softly.

She turned back to her husband. I could see her talking quietly and forcefully to him. Saw him nod his head several times.

***

Twenty minutes later we landed at Mfuwe on the border of the South Luangwa Park.

While Garth filed his flight plan for our onward journey, I accompanied the couple to the edge of the airstrip. A driver from one of the upmarket lodges in the park was waiting for them.

'Son,' the man said as he shook my hand, 'you just let me know if I can be of assistance with this poaching atrocity.' He handed me a business card with a handwritten local number on it.

'You just call me.' It came out as an order.

I looked at the card. I did not recognise the name, but I did recognise the title. **CHAIRMAN OF THE JOINT CHIEFS OF STAFF USMC.** The highest-ranking military commander in the United States Department of Defence.

No wonder the ambassador had been his personal taxi driver.

As Garth and I flew on to North Luangwa, I wondered what faced us ahead.

Animals butchered for their tusks are not scenes for the faint-hearted. I had seen tough, hard-bitten men, both white and black, weep at the sight.

And then Beth had also said, 'Much more.' What had she meant by that?

Beth was hard to know yet easy to love. Various men, and women, had fallen for her. She spurned them all. Her passion was reserved for the bush, for the conservation of Africa's wild animals, for the study and research into their continued survival.

She was the only daughter of a white Zimbabwean citrus farmer. One of many farmers whose land had been seized by black squatters claiming to be freedom fighters. Under their occupation the orchards had withered and died where they stood. Vast acres of dead trees turned into tombstones, ending generations of endeavour and self-sufficiency.

When you first met Beth you saw a fair-haired and fair-skinned woman. Shapely and attractive in an understated way, with grey piercing eyes that never seemed to blink.

Beth had grown up dogged and tough. She could drive an excavator, fix a broken water pump, service a Land Rover and shoot like a champion. She was a crack markswoman, a sharpshooter of the highest order and skill; long range, large bore, hand guns - it made no difference.

And yet there was also a vulnerability to her. It occurred to me that she could be slightly autistic. She would at times appear anti-social, aloof, slow to make friends, slow to accept friendships.

Close friends of mine, both men and women, who also knew her, would sometimes say that they thought Beth was secretly in love with me.

My own feelings for her were deep, untested, the invisible barrier around her difficult to penetrate. Never once had she shown or demonstrated any close affection to me. However, I had noticed that when we were in the company of others she would often try to sit or stand next to me. Never once had we touched one another, not even the most cursory contact.

Her characteristics were like that of a leopard. Cautious and wary in social gatherings, confident and adept in her bush surroundings.

***

The scene that Beth led us to was one of brutal horror.

Standing there, looking on in dismay, I could hear the plaintive call of a red-chested cuckoo, its sound a sad lament to the outrage facing us.

For some unknown and peculiar reason Samson and Hercules had been killed less than three hundred metres apart. It was very unusual to find both great animals so close together in that immense wilderness.

Spread around the bodies were large patches of gore and blood. The stench was ferocious. Hyenas, jackals and vultures had been gorging on the carcasses; for the moment our presence had chased them away.

Where the poachers had hacked the horn and tusks out, the mutilation to the poor animals' heads was too appalling to look at.

Then Beth said something very strange: 'This is just the beginning.'

Garth and I stared at her. Her eyes were like stone. And yet I could see a sensitive quiver around her lips. As if she wanted to cry but was determined not to.

And then Beth did something even stranger. She clasped my left hand.

With her rifle slung over her left shoulder she led me into the bush. Garth followed behind. Nobody said a word.

We came out onto a track that had been cut as a firebreak. Turning northwards we continued to follow it for about fifteen minutes.

There were noises ahead. Grunting and odd maniacal giggles slowly growing louder.

'More hyenas,' I said aloud.

Beth lifted her rifle. Shouted loudly. Fired a single shot into the air.

The noises stopped. She fired again. We could hear some clattering sounds as the scavengers scurried off across the stony verges.

Five bodies lay in the track. Or rather the remains of five bodies. Most were missing body parts. Two of the torsos were also headless. Entrails were strewn around, the foul smell of rapidly putrefying faeces overpowering in the humid air. The hyenas had been busy.

'What the fuck happened here?' Garth gasped.

I already knew the answer. This was the *'much more'*.

I squatted down to examine the first corpse. Beth bent down alongside me, still holding my hand tightly.

The bullet hole was just above the nasal bone right between the man's eyes. Most of the back of his head been blown away. He had died instantly.

The next two bodies were the same. A single shot to the head. Instantaneous death. The fourth and fifth I couldn't determine; the missing heads were nowhere to be found. Behind us I could hear Garth retching, then being violently sick.

'Whew!' I exhaled, standing up slowly and stretching.

I studied Beth carefully. Tears were running down her cheeks, but she remained composed. I touched her shoulder, drew her slightly closer.

'I...caught them...head on. Four men, in pairs. Carrying Hercules' tusks. The fifth man at the back had Samson's horn on his head.' She shuddered. 'It was so...blatant...so awful!'

'Let's stand in the shade over there while we decide what to do next,' I said. 'Wait for Garth to recover.'

'Shaun...Shaun?' Her voice was ominously low. She looked close to collapse, yet her hand still gripped mine strongly.

'Yes?'

'We...we need to walk on.'

'I think we should do something with these bodies first.'

'Please, Shaun. We need to walk on.' She sounded more desperate now as she pulled me forward.

The track widened slightly as we made our way along it. In the distance I thought I could see a vehicle. We drew steadily closer.

I could also see something else - an ungainly heap sprawled in the sand.

Uncertain, cautious, I wanted to slow down, to stop. But Beth tugged me on.

The vehicle was an expensive black Range Rover. It appeared to be official. Whether it belonged to the government, an embassy, or a non-governmental agency was uncertain. The number plate was missing.

Somebody must have removed it.

I held back and made Beth stop.

In some incongruous and ironic similarity to where the poachers had been killed, I could now hear a black cuckoo calling. In contrast to the scene, its call sounded somewhat cheery.

Slowly we moved forward. Very slowly I examined another violent scene.

'The buyers,' Beth murmured. 'They were waiting here. For the poachers. But…'

'But?' I asked.

'I got here first.'

She had used more than one bullet on each victim.

A wild red mist must have descended on her. Her anger terrible and uncontrolled, her rifle set on semi-automatic. All the windows of the Range Rover were completely shattered. Shards of mirror and glass lay strewn around. One of the car tyres was in shreds.

Inside the vehicle were two bodies, seemingly of Chinese origin. Once clad in beige long trousered safari suits, they were now drenched in blood. Both men had died of multiple bullet wounds.

The same was true of the man who lay in front of the vehicle. He appeared to have been well groomed and expensively dressed. Now he was covered in sand and flies and blackening blood.

'Look around the back,' Beth said harshly. 'Come with me.'

We pushed through the surrounding bush. She pointed to a fourth body lying face down.

'Precious,' Beth whispered. 'She was in on all of this.'

The young woman appeared to have been running away; she had made less than ten metres. I could see six bullet holes stitched down the back of her T-shirt.

We returned to the front of the car.

'I also found this…' Beth said shakily. Reaching under the front seat, she took out a large brown envelope. I opened it. Inside were wads of US dollars bound together with elastic bands.

Carefully I looked around. 'Is there anyone else here?' I asked.

'No,' she answered. 'I think the nearest people at the moment are some subsistence farmers, Tonga people. They're about twelve kilometres away.'

'And the local rangers?'

'Conveniently sent to Lavusi Manda,' she said grimly. 'They left two days ago.'

Garth came over to us. He looked pale and shaken but seemed to be under control.

'Fuck, man,' he said hoarsely. 'We seem to have a slight problem.'

Coarse and droll, at any other time or under other circumstances his words might have been amusing. But facing us was a very serious and dangerous situation.

Beth had killed nine people. In two separate incidents. Less than two kilometres apart. A white woman had killed six black African men, one black African woman and two Chinese nationals. In Zambia. An official looking top-of-the-range vehicle was beyond repair, riddled with bullet holes.

The repercussions would be enormous.

The fact that two great animals had also lost their lives would be conveniently overlooked. Hercules and Samson would become insignificant and irrelevant.

**

The minister looked surly and gave the appearance of bored arrogance as he slouched in his chair.

'Thank you for meeting with us.' Bluff and affable, the US ambassador was just the opposite.

'Fifteen minutes,' the minister said shortly. 'That is all.'

'Let me start then.' Under the ambassador's affability lay an edge of steel.

'No, let me start,' the minister interrupted. 'Why did you ask for this meeting? At such short notice. And why did you insist that I have my deputy here and the head of the Zambian Wildlife Authority? And who are these people with you?' A wide, rude gesture seemed to encompass us all.

'I think,' and now the ambassador's voice had hardened significantly, 'once you have heard what we are about to tell you, you may reconsider the time allocated for this meeting.'

160

'What…what are you saying?' The minister spluttered.

Ambassador Patterson was unperturbed. 'We think that your co-operation and understanding will be of great benefit. Both to the Zambian government and to your own Ministry of Environmental Protection in particular.'

'Do you know who I am?' The man smirked. 'I sit at the president's table. That is who I am.'

Ignoring the rhetorical question, Patterson continued. 'First let me introduce my colleagues. This is Dr Shaun Brotherton who works at the Eye Hospital here in Lusaka. And next to him is General Paul Stafford, recently retired Commanding General of our Defence Department.'

The minister sat more upright, clearly surprised.

'What is this all about?' he asked.

'Well, it would be useful for you to introduce your colleagues.' The ambassador smiled disarmingly. 'But I believe they are Mr Tembo and Mr Mgando; is that correct?'

The two men, one on either side of the minister, both nodded.

'Good,' Ambassador Patterson went on. 'I think we should keep the discussion off the record. Can you switch off the equipment, please? And I suggest we leave our cell phones outside, also switched off. Maybe your secretary could deal with that?'

The minister looked nonplussed but the ambassador was not to be deterred.

The secretary was duly summoned. On the minister's instruction she switched off the recording equipment and took all the phones to her office.

'Maybe at the end of our meeting, if we reach a suitable agreement,' Patterson's gaze went around the table, 'your secretary can arrange for one of the government attorneys to draft an appropriate document for us to sign. Perhaps she could forewarn them now?'

'What agreement? We do not even know what you want!' the minister said loudly.

Patterson just smiled. 'That's okay. Let me lay out the problem for you. You may already be familiar with a few of the facts.'

161

His face turned grim. 'Four days ago, just after sunrise, five poachers were apprehended in the North Luangwa Park. They had just killed the largest male elephant and the only known adult male rhino in the park.'

Nobody said a word. There was a look of dismay on the ZAWA chief's face.

'Then, less than an hour later, four more individuals, including two Chinese men and a Zambian woman, were confronted. They were the buyers waiting for the poachers.'

The minister turned to his colleagues. 'You know of this?' he asked.

Both shook their heads, obviously disconcerted.

'We know Zambia has a poaching problem,' the minister said. 'We are trying our best to control it.' Then a thought struck him. 'You mentioned four people - two Chinese, one woman. Who is the fourth?'

'Was, Mr Minister.'

'Was? What are you saying?'

'The local newspapers are reporting that the president's son-in-law has gone missing.' The ambassador's voice had a severe accusing edge to it. 'His wife, the president's first-born, is very worried. She has not seen or heard from him in four days.'

'Mr Patterson,' the head of ZAWA spoke for the first time. 'Why are you being mysterious? What are you insinuating?'

The ambassador didn't reply. Instead he reached into his jacket pocket and took out a folded sheet of paper. He placed it on the table in front of the three officials.

The minister opened the paper and scrutinised it, then passed it to the man on his right.

'Miriam!' the minister shouted. 'Miriam!'

The secretary opened the door. 'Yes, sir?'

'Bring tea. And cancel all my other meetings for the day. Now!'

'Yes, sir.' She scooted out.

'This is a copy of the man's driver's licence,' the minister stated. 'What is this supposed to mean?'

'It means that we have the original licence. Plus we have the passports of the Chinese nationals,' the ambassador replied.

'Mr Patterson, my colleague said that you were mysterious. I think you're being obscure and I'm finding this very frustrating. What is going on?'

'Right; let me tell you.' The ambassador's eyes were implacable. 'The five poachers, the two Chinese, the president's son-in-law and a young woman were all apprehended and killed at the scene of the poaching. For your information, the woman is also related to the president. One of his nieces, in fact.'

For a moment there was total silence.

Hesitantly, then angrily, the head of ZAWA spoke. 'Nine people? Nine people were killed in my park? A park under my department's control! That is impossible! And intolerable! We know nothing of this!'

The man glared around the table. 'We will bring these killers to the courts. We do not allow an eye for an eye here; we do not allow rogue justice. We are a civilised nation.'

His tirade was interrupted by the return of the minister's secretary. With a clatter she placed the tray on the table and began to set out the cups and saucers.

'Miriam, we will pour our own tea, thank you,' the minister said. 'Please leave us and close the door. We are not to be disturbed.'

He waited until she had left before speaking again. 'This is a very bad event, Mr Patterson. You are,' he chose the word carefully, 'suggesting that those high up in power are benefitting from the poaching of our wild animals.'

'Yes,' the ambassador said firmly. 'And there is something else.' He took more folded papers from his jacket pocket. 'The buyers were in an official car, one belonging to the president's office. To his fleet.'

He opened the documents and handed them over.

The three officials studied them carefully.

'Are you saying that this vehicle is somehow implicated?' the minister asked.

'Yes,' Patterson stated. 'The president's son-in-law was driving it.'

'You are sure?'

'Absolutely. We have the logbook and all the records that were in it.'

163

'And where is the car now?'

'It has been destroyed.'

'What?' the minister exclaimed. 'That car must be worth more than US$100 000!'

Lifting his teacup to his lips, the ambassador shrugged his shoulders and said nothing more.

The minister turned to his colleagues. There was rapid discussion in Bemba; the only English word that didn't get translated was *confidential*.

The third man who had as yet not said anything, suddenly spoke. 'Mr Ambassador, you will need to tell us who killed these nine people. We need to know.' He glared across the table and stood up, pointing his finger. 'Did this general and this doctor do it? Is that why they are here? Did they kill them?'

'No, son,' the general answered directly. 'Sit down. We are not your problem.' His eyes, and his voice, were as cold as ice. 'We are your solution.'

***

We worked at fever pitch to clear up.

First Garth and I loaded the two bodies into the back of the Range Rover to join their Chinese accomplices.

I started the car. Luckily none of the bullets that Beth had fired seemed to have damaged the engine mechanically. Slowly I drove back down the track to where the other five bodies lay, the vehicle lurching on its destroyed tyre.

Behind us Beth removed as much of the debris as she could. She picked up every piece of broken glass and plastic. Knowing how many bullets she had originally loaded, she searched for the empty casings. Only two could not be found.

Probably lodged in the vehicle somewhere, she thought.

In order to eradicate as much of the trace evidence and bloodstains as possible, she made small fires over the areas where the man and Precious had bled into the ground.

Then, with a leafy branch cut from a miombo bush and a hand-broom made from some tufted grass, she carefully swept and brushed the area. She was so thorough that by the time she had finished the area bore no evidence of the firefight.

Severe rain and wind were forecast for the next twenty-four hours. If the bad weather arrived early it would be a bonus; any remaining traces would soon be eliminated.

After a final scout around, she strode off to where Garth and I were busy.

We built a huge funeral pyre. I was left to drag the bodies of the poachers nearer and gather the loose body parts together.

'Shit, I don't know how you can do this, man,' Garth muttered.

'Even though I'm a doctor, this is just as hard for me,' I responded.

'Fuck, I'm sorry, man,' Garth turned away; he could not watch. 'I can't help you. I'll be sick again.' He gagged and started to dry-retch.

'Don't worry. Can you get some petrol out of the car? We need to douse everything before lighting it.'

'No problem.' Doing things with his hands came easily to Garth.

There was a full toolbox in the back of Beth's small truck plus a few empty containers that were used for spare fuel and water. Within minutes Garth had filled them with fuel from the Range Rover's tank.

I stacked the pyre higher and higher, and when Beth returned she helped me lay the bodies on it. Over the bodies we piled more logs and brushwood. Adjacent to the heap we built a separate hoard of timber in reserve.

We did the same with the Range Rover, filling the interior with timber, pushing smaller logs and dry grass under the vehicle, then placing more broken branches and grass over it.

Then, as best we could, we cleared a firebreak around the area. The track was bone dry which helped.

Every so often I glanced at Beth as she helped me. Each time she gave me a small taut smile; she was holding herself tightly under control.

I wondered what lay ahead for her. For us.

The air was pungent with the smell of petrol as Garth began to sprinkle it across the two heaps. He had plaited some very dry grass into a loosely woven rope, creating a primitive detonating cord, then he splashed a little petrol over that too.

165

The last thing he did was deflate the vehicle's tyres.

'I think it's time to light this lot,' I said.

We moved well away and Garth lit the rope. There was an initial smoky splutter and then, flaring sharply, the rope caught fire.

The heaps exploded into an instantaneous conflagration. We had to move even further back. And as the flames and heat built in intensity, so did the stench - a vile mixture of raging rubber and plastic and roasting human flesh.

There is no worse smell than that of human flesh burning.

Beth had taken my hand again. Her face pressed into my shoulder, she turned away from the gruesome spectacle. Garth couldn't watch either.

'Why don't the two of you do a slow patrol around the area,' I said. 'Make sure there is nobody else here. Then head back to camp and get cleaned up.'

'What about you?' Beth asked softly.

'In an hour or so it will be getting dark. Come back in your car. Maybe bring some coffee and we'll wait this out - keep the fires burning until everything is destroyed.'

There was an incandescent roar as something in the Range Rover exploded.

'We'll come back again in the morning and clear up some more. As long as there is still no-one else here.'

I turned from one friend to the other. Both Garth and Beth looked totally exhausted. Their faces were drawn and filthy, etched with the shock of what had happened. Etched with the implications of what we had done.

I must have looked just the same.

***

I stood there with the sun not yet risen. The air was warm and humid, dense, unusual for so early in the day. The early morning birds were twittering. In the far-off distance I heard a lion roar, and then again. *Must be a kill.*

The Range Rover was completely destroyed. Lumpy pieces of molten metal and glass lay in the sand. Everything combustible was gone; all that was left intact was the chassis and engine block.

The heat had been so intense that of the four bodies in the vehicle, only a few very small pieces of charred bone and a little ash remained. Carefully I brushed these into a plastic bucket.

The funeral pyre was completely burnt down. A few fragments lay in the cinders and I scooped those into the bucket too. I would dispose of them later.

There was little more that could be done.

I felt the first drops of rain, could see a heavy cloud fast approaching from the northeast. I turned and walked swiftly back to camp, running the last section as the rain began to teem down.

Beth was waiting for me. Garth had left at first light to fly back to Lusaka. I kissed her gently and she seemed to melt into me.

I sat at the table while she made coffee. Neither of us spoke. She brought the cup over and kissed me again.

All night while I kept the fires going my thoughts had been difficult to consolidate. What to do next? Who should I go to for advice? Should I report it to the authorities? Should we all remain quiet and see what happened next? These thoughts and many more had circulated through my mind.

Finally I knew the only option open to us.

I took the general's business card from my pocket and picked up the satellite phone, then carefully dialled the handwritten number on it.

***

The team setting out for patrol was ready. I watched as they checked their weapons and equipment; they had been drilled and trained to military precision. Their vehicles were equally impressive. Modern and up to date, the vehicles had evolved from the Iraq and Afghanistan conflicts and were perfectly suited for the terrain in Luangwa. They were also equipped with the latest in communication systems and drone surveillance.

The man in command was an iron-hard Afro-American from Alabama. Gilbert Jones had seen service in more dangerous areas than most — Colombia, Iraq, Afghanistan, Mali, Congo. He volunteered when others didn't want to.

But now he was here.

Under the control of General Stafford (rtd) he now headed up the North Luangwa Anti-Poaching Unit. His secondment from the US Marine Corps would last for five years.

On the odd occasion when Gilbert relaxed, a shot glass of neat bourbon in his hand, he would chat to me in his soft southern drawl. 'This is the best assignment I have ever had; feels like early retirement.' Or: 'This is like my honeymoon with my first wife. That was tough but, like here, nobody shot back at me.' Then he would grin. 'Just don't you tell the general that! He'll think I'm getting soft and arrange for me to be sent to hell and gone again.'

Up at the main gate to the park a small clinic had been built. Well-stocked and well-equipped, that was where I now worked. Two local women were in training as nurse-aides.

The funding to establish and sustain the clinic had been substantial. An underlying endowment meant that I could work there for the next five years as well.

General Stafford had used his considerable influence and contacts, and the United States and Zambian governments had struck a deal.

Since becoming my wife Beth had blossomed. Her conservation and research projects were also now well supported. Garth had been the best man at our wedding. However, seeing as there was minimal probability of him being sober and refraining from profanity, he had agreed he would not make a speech. Ambassador Patterson had enjoyed being in charge.

In their innocence Hercules and Samson had left a legacy; their terrible deaths had not been totally in vain.

THE GIRL FROM CALVINIA

South Africa 2014

My wife looked tense standing in the early morning queue. The line to clear customs at the OR Tambo Airport in Johannesburg zig-zagged its way from side to side. There must have been at least eighty people ahead of us.

Jeannie's eyes flickered continuously. I could see that something was disturbing her. She had been the same on the flight over from England - restless, couldn't settle, irritable, and even seemed angry at me.

On the plane I asked her what the problem was, but irascibly she replied, 'I just can't get comfortable.'

It appeared to me to be more than that.

We were returning to Africa for the first time in nearly twelve years. Our destination was Botswana to visit my brother who had set up a small eco-lodge on the Moremi Park border. The plan was to hire a car in Johannesburg, drive to Gaborone and then on to Maun where Alan would meet us.

I was excited to be back in Africa again after so long, and eager for Jeannie to meet my family. They had never met her because we had married quietly in England seven years before.

But standing there my excitement steadily lessened, turning to worry.

There were small beads of sweat on Jeannie's upper lip and she appeared pale. I could see her hands shaking. There definitely appeared to be something wrong. Perhaps she was falling ill.

Eventually we were at the front of the queue.

I went first. The customs official asked a few perfunctory questions, tapped his keyboard, stamped my passport and waved me through.

Waiting on the other side of the counters, I watched as Jeannie stood there. The questions posed seemed to be more detailed and lengthy. I saw her shake her head and point to me, her anxiety evident.

The official called someone over, a supervisor of some sort. They scanned Jeannie's passport again, then both shook their heads. After a short discussion they let her through, but did not return her passport.

The officials joined us.

'What's the problem?' I asked.

'There is a problem with this lady's passport,' the supervisor replied sharply.

'What problem?'

'Come with us, please.'

'What about our luggage?'

There was further discussion between the two men. They spoke in Sotho; I couldn't understand a word.

'We will help you collect your bags. But you must come with us.'

'What is going on?' I asked Jeannie.

'I don't know.' Her eyes would not meet mine.

The white-cold look on her face startled me; I had never seen it before. Brooding rage overlying fear. And it felt directed at me.

Our bags were located and loaded on to a trolley. Then we were ushered through a door marked 'Staff Only' and led through winding passages to a small unoccupied office. One of the officials remained with us, the other, our passports in hand, disappeared into the apparent maze.

I took Jeannie's hand to hold it and offer support, but she abruptly withdrew and shook her head.

My mind spun, trying to grasp the situation. The beautiful, loving and happy woman I had married seemed to have changed into some distant stranger. I just could not work it out. She appeared to be directing waves of blame at me for reasons I couldn't fathom.

We continued to sit there, the waiting interminable.

The official with us remained totally unresponsive. He played on his mobile phone, sending innumerable text messages.

I looked at my watch. An hour and a half had passed since we'd been detained at the customs desk. I stood up and went to the door.

'No. Sit down. Wait.' The official's voice was gruff and aggressive. He half stood, pointing to my chair.

'Just tell us what is going on,' I spluttered.

'Sit down. Wait.'

Ten minutes later the door opened. A strongly built white man in a rumpled dark suit entered the room. Immediately behind him followed a slender uniformed police woman carrying an extra chair. They dismissed the customs official and sat down at the desk to face us.

The white man spoke first. 'I am Detective Inspector Jan du Plessis and this is my colleague Constable Leah Mbula.' His voice was curt and authoritative.

He made to address himself to me first, but my impatience spilled over. 'What the hell is going on?'

He looked at me evenly. 'You are Dr Mathee. Dr Steven Mathee?'

'Yes,' I replied shortly.

'We are investigating charges that may involve your wife.'

'What?'

'I would appreciate you answering only two questions at this time,' he went on. 'If the answers are as I expect, you will be free to go.'

'And my wife, too?'

'No. We wish to interview her thoroughly. We are making the necessary arrangements.'

'But...but we are British citizens. Surely we are allowed legal representation.' I searched for something else. 'And consular representation!'

The detective shook his head. 'I work for Interpol, not the South African Police. Believe me, we have all the authority necessary to detain your wife.'

The atmosphere in the room was charged, like the pause between two lightning strikes.

Jeannie sat pale and unmoving, withdrawn deep into herself. She glared at me with what I could only interpret as venomous enmity.

My mind was filled with apprehension and uncertainty.

'I need to go to the toilet.' Jeannie's voice sounded strained and tense.

The policeman studied her carefully.

'Please, Detective Inspector,' she tried again, her tone more polite. 'I really need to go. Maybe you could question Steven in the meantime.' She turned to the policewoman, slightly imploring, clearly trying to obtain a little sympathy. 'Please!'

'Go with her,' Du Plessis gestured. He waited until they had left the room, removed a small notebook from his pocket and turned to me.

'Dr Mathee, could you explain to me when and where you met your wife?'

'We met in Oxford, England. She attended a lecture I was giving. That was in 2006.'

He wrote in his book. 'And...when did you get married?'

'We went out for a year. Married in 2007.'

'Hmmm...there is one more question. How much do you know of her past? That is, before she met you.'

'Very little. She has never spoken of it. It is the unwritten rule.'

'What do you mean by that?' he asked.

'It was her condition. I was never to ask of her past - her life in South Africa prior to immigrating to England. She said that if I was prepared to accept that, accept her in the here and now, then she would go out with me.'

'And, of course, you agreed,' he stated bluntly.

'Wouldn't you? Look at her - beautiful, intelligent, fifteen years younger than me. We were both single. Wouldn't you have done the same thing?'

The policeman stared at me, his face openly sceptical. 'I always thought that respect and honesty were the foundation stones of marriage. I'm afraid your wife has failed you in this.'

I wanted to respond as a flare of anger arose within me.

He raised his hand. 'That is all, Dr Mathee. As soon as my colleague returns she will take you to the Executive Lounge.'

'And?'

'The UK Embassy in Pretoria is sending someone down to help you. I have already spoken to them.'

'I'm not sure I understand. What about my wife?' My anger was building, but somehow I kept it under control.

'Dr Mathee,' he said grimly, 'we are taking her into custody. The representative from the embassy will explain everything to you.'

'Are you really allowed to? I mean legally, legitimately?' I asked again.

'Doctor, I have already explained. I have the authority.' He bent to his notebook, the scratching of his pen the only sound in the room. Then he glanced at his watch. A frown appeared on his face.

He stood and went to the door, opened it and looked down the passage. There appeared to be a flurry of activity. A clamour of voices could be heard.

Somebody shouted: 'Where is that policeman?'

Detective Inspector du Plessis called back. 'Here!'

The voice shouted again. 'Come quickly. There is big trouble.'

He turned to me. 'Come with me. Stay close. Don't give me problems, too.'

I followed him down the passage to where a group of people stood bunched at a doorway. Du Plessis took my arm and pushed his way through.

'In there.' A woman, one hand to her face, pointed. 'It's terrible.'

The sight facing us was like a scene from some gory horror film. The policewoman sat half slumped in a corner. She appeared to have been repeatedly bludgeoned by the lid of a toilet seat. The seat was now jammed over her head and neck in a tight-fitting trap.

Blood poured from deep gashes in her head and another even deeper to her throat. Her face had been ripped to shreds by the force of the assault. Blood pooled around her, seeping into her clothes and shoes.

From where I stood, she appeared to be fatally unconscious, close to death.

'Can you help her, Doctor?' The policeman's heavy demeanour was filled with alarm.

I shook my head. 'No, I can't. I'm a scientist, not a medical doctor.'

My head reeled as I absorbed the scene in all its appalling detail. The realisation slowly sank in that Jeannie, my wife, had done this.

I sank to my haunches, shocked and faint.

***

She sat at a small circular table in the bar area.

Her mind had changed into another gear, a low drive that calculated through torque and power.

What had happened during the last five hours was already slipping into the recess in her brain. A recess which harboured memories she seldom brought back: her husband for the last seven years, the man who had given her so much. The quiet, peaceful, controlled life in England. Her few friends and work colleagues. The attack on the thin policewoman in the airport building.

All now submerged to be forgotten.

Stirring the Campari and soda in front of her, she looked around as she planned her next move.

She knew she had been fortunate. Getting from the toilet where the stricken policewoman lay to the airport's exit had taken less than a minute - through two doors also marked 'Staff Only', straight into the throng of people in the arrivals hall.

At the waiting stand the Hilton Hotel courtesy shuttle bus stood ready to depart. She hopped in just as the driver was about to close the door.

Five minutes later she was dropped off. She waited in the hotel's foyer until the bus departed on the next shuttle, then she went outside and looked around. There were two hotels across the road, the second some 400 metres from the first.

She made her way into the nearest hotel and found the ladies' change room. There she removed her jacket and loosened the shirt waist. Padding the jacket around herself, she looked in the mirror and made a few adjustments. After wetting her hair lightly she swung it over her left eye in a continental fashion. Using her fingernails as a makeshift comb, she managed to roughly achieve the look she wanted. Finally she bent down and slipped a thick wad of toilet paper into her left shoe.

A slightly flustered, dumpy woman limped into the next hotel down the road.

Then, the disguise reversed, she went to the bar and ordered a single drink. The money in the policewoman's purse would cover no more.

She sat watching the guests and their visitors come and go. Taking her time, she weighed them up carefully.

The man she selected looked to be in his late fifties, overweight but neatly dressed. Clothes well-worn, if a little old-fashioned.

A travelling salesman or maybe an agricultural representative, she mused.

He finished the beer in front of him and made his way into the hotel's restaurant.

When he was out of view, she followed him in. She looked around and then took the table facing him. She waited until they had both ordered and he had his next drink in front of him, before speaking.

'I know it's a bit forward,' she said, 'but we seem to be the only people on our own here. Would you like to join me?' She gestured at the chair next to her.

The man seemed a little surprised. 'Madam,' his English heavily accented, 'that is very gracious.' He stood and extended his hand. 'Ben van Tonder.'

'And I am Joanne Oxenford,' she responded.

***

Surreptitiously, her top button undone, she reeled him in slowly and steadily.

His stories interested her. She giggled at his little jokes, raised her eyebrows in mock surprise at those more risqué.

They dawdled over dinner. A bottle of wine arrived. She nursed a glass, he drank the rest.

The evening needed to move forward.

'I need to freshen up. I'll be back in a few minutes.'

She stood and stretched evocatively. His look moved to her breasts; she could feel his eyes on her as she made her way across the room.

He smiled as she returned.

'Shall we settle the bill?'

'My dear, I have already done that.'

'I can't let you pay for me.' She made to open the stolen purse.

'No, no, it's my pleasure. This has been such a delightful evening, after all.'

His gait slightly unsteady, she walked with him to the lifts.

Hesitantly he turned to her. 'Do you...do you want another drink?' he asked. 'A little nightcap?'

She took her time before replying, touching his arm. 'Yes, why not. But let's go to one of our rooms. I really need to put my feet up.'

'There is a mini-bar in mine.' His voice was now less tentative, underlying desire making it slightly hoarse.

***

Pillows behind her back, she sat propped up on the bed, watching and scheming as he moved about the dimmed room.

'Why don't we shower first?' she suggested, opening another button on her blouse.

He nodded, his face flushing with lust.

Turning, he emptied his pockets. Her eyes carefully took note of where he placed his car keys and wallet.

'You go. I'll follow in a minute.' She undid another button.

Her mind weighed the options. The first was to leave as soon as he started showering - take the keys and make a dash for it.

'Patience,' her brain said. 'You need more time. Take the other option.'

His upper body was pale and stoutly solid. Around his waist the muscularity was softening into fat. She concealed a small shudder as he stripped - his buttocks loose and flabby in his underpants.

She saw him stagger as he hung his trousers over the chair. An evening of alcohol had taken effect. Logically she knew that the shower might revive him. She would have to tire him out quickly. Maybe the excitement of intense and surprising sex would do that.

He filled the cubicle through the translucent glass, his body singularly unattractive, sallow and overweight. She opened the shower door. Her nudity made him gasp.

'Turn around, then we can both fit in,' she murmured, pressing into the shower behind him. That way he would not see the look of revulsion on her face.

His erect stubby penis brushed her hand. She grasped it and milked him firmly, the soapy foam mixing with his semen as he abruptly came in shuddering grunts.

She held on to him and slowly started the action again. It took longer this time. Her free hand moved over him, through his legs, around his chest, pinching his nipples between thumb and forefinger. Reaching higher, her teeth nipped his earlobes.

'My God,' he panted. 'My God!' He ejaculated again as sensation overtook him.

She backed away, hands on his arms. He turned to try and kiss her. She avoided the emotional gratitude in his eyes.

'Let me shower. You go to bed; I'll join you in a few minutes.'

She drew out the shower, took time in drying her hair.

When she emerged he was already dozing, almost asleep, totally spent by what had just happened. She crept in next to him and lay there, eyes open in the darkened room. Waiting. Planning.

She touched his shoulder. There was no response. His snoring became deeper. Easing away, she slipped out of the bed and dressed quickly.

Shoes in one hand, his wallet and car keys in the other, she quietly opened the room door and looked out. The passage was deserted. She stopped. Listened. The snoring continued uninterrupted.

Leaving the door slightly ajar, she ran lightly along the passage, down the fire escape stairs, through the now vacant foyer and out into the carpark.

There were about twenty cars. She looked around and pressed the immobiliser button on the key. There was an audible '*click*'. In the third bay away from her, the rear lights on a white Toyota

Hilux SUV flashed. Holding her breath, she grasped the handle and opened the car door, half expecting the alarm to sound.

Nothing happened.

The woman got in and switched on the ignition. The engine sounded smooth and powerful. Taking a moment to gather her bearings, she sat back and fastened the seatbelt.

Slowly she drove to the exit. A sleepy security guard lifted the access boom and waved her through. Turning out of the carpark she accelerated steadily, following the road signs.

The north/south freeway lay directly ahead. At two in the morning there was hardly any traffic. She pulled into a lay-by and studied the gauges. The fuel tank indicated 'full' and the others all appeared normal.

She opened the man's wallet. There were three credit cards, a fuel card, driver's licence, and a thick wad of large denomination banknotes.

'That will keep me going,' she said to herself. She kept the fuel- and credit cards, but threw the licence out the window.

Adjusting the seat forward a fraction, she made herself comfortable and looked in the mirror. The person looking back at her was the only one she had trusted ever since childhood.

She drove forward. Swung left onto the freeway. Headed south.

***

I sat in the Executive Lounge and waited. There was little else I could do. Desultorily I paged through magazines and newspapers. Drank one cup of coffee after the next.

Just before five o'clock in the afternoon a woman came into the room and spoke to the attendant. A few words were exchanged. She made her way over to me.

'Dr Mathee?' she enquired.

'Yes.'

'I am Mary Warren, from the British Embassy. Here is my card.' She was short and fair and very English.

'I am at a complete loss…' My voice shook slightly.

'I understand.' Her voice was brisk, but not without sympathy.

'What am I supposed to do…my passport? My baggage? My wife? I have been here all day and I don't know what is going on.'

'I understand,' she said again. 'Detective Inspector du Plessis has agreed that we will look after you. We are to report back to him at eleven o'clock tomorrow morning.'

'And then?'

'He will bring us up to date.'

'Do you know what my wife has done?'

Mary shook her head. 'Only a few brief details.'

The look on my face made her carry on. 'All I am allowed to tell you is that there is a long outstanding warrant for your wife's arrest. And, obviously, after what has happened here today, further charges are to be laid.'

'What is the outstanding warrant for?' I asked.

'Dr Mathee, I'm not sure that I should be the one telling you this, but…' she saw the worry on my face. 'Your wife is wanted for murder.'

'Murder!'

'Yes, there are…' she searched for the appropriate words, 'there are multiple charges.'

I sat there stunned.

'We need to go now; please follow me. I cannot tell you anymore because I do not know anymore.'

***

I spent most of the night awake. Not only because of what had happened during the last twenty-four hours, but also because I was trying to understand what had happened during the years I had been with Jeannie.

Everything had been ordinary. At least that was what I had always felt. We were a quiet married couple going about the normalities of everyday life.

I could recall occasional moments when I had felt that she became detached and distant, but that would soon fade and she would return to being with me.

My thoughts kept churning around and around. Exhausted I eventually drifted off to sleep, but my mind remained active with dreams intense and in turmoil.

In one scene, sharp and short-lived, I could see her. Jeannie appeared without clothes on. Somewhere near water. Visions of a rapidly flowing river. She stood at its head under a waterfall, slowly disappearing from view.

Startled, I awoke.

The dream had seemed so vivid, the image of her as real as could be. It was as if she were in the room with me.

Switching on the light, I peered at my watch.

The dial reflected one thirty in the morning.

***

Detective Inspector du Plessis looked tired. Clearly he had not slept much either.

We sat in his office. I saw then that his slightly rumpled appearance was deceptive. It was more due to overwork and fatigue than sloppiness. His office was fastidiously tidy. Pictures had been hung with thought and precision on the walls, a photograph of Nelson Mandela prominently displayed. His case files were carefully stacked, with Post-It notes in various colours lodged neatly at places within them.

A thick solitary file lay on the desk directly in front of him. I knew whose it was. Its bulkiness surprised me.

He gestured for Mary and me to sit.

'Dr Mathee, I have advised Miss Warren that we need to take a statement from you. After that you will be free to go.'

'But my passport?'

Opening a desk drawer, he reached in and took out the passport, then passed it across the desk to me.

'After I give my statement are you prepared to tell me what my wife is accused of? Prior to yesterday, of course,' I added quickly.

'I will tell you whatever you want to know,' he replied. 'However, it's a story you may wish you'd never heard.'

Jeannie's real name was Jolene van der Walt. She had grown up in the small town of Calvinia some two hundred and fifty kilometres north of Cape Town. The only child of a neurotic alcoholic mother and an overbearing jealous father. A clever girl, she completed school and moved to Cape Town, gaining entrance at the University of Cape Town to study a BSc degree.

The first two years passed smoothly. Introverted and serious, she studied hard and kept to herself. She ignored her fellow female students and found the male students boorish and immature. During the holidays she worked part-time wherever she could. Tried at all costs to avoid going home to her parents.

Then she fell in love.

Midway through her third year, and just after her twenty-first birthday, she took a temporary job for a month at a small dental practice. The affair that she and the already married dentist embarked on was like a wildfire that exploded out of all control.

Their motives for this conflagration were totally different. Dirk van Heerden just wanted her because she was attractive, sexually pliable and always available. Her young and willing firm body kept him in a state of constant arousal. When she went back to university he planned to drop her and look for someone else. But Jolene wanted him permanently. His local status and affluence would be hers to dominate and control. His wife and children were merely pawns to be discarded.

Their downfall came one weekend.

Van Heerden's unsuspecting wife had taken the children to visit their grandparents. The illicit lovers had the time to themselves. Jolene stayed overnight. Friday night stretched into Saturday, and then into Sunday. She toyed with her older lover. They had sex in the marriage bed, over a chair in the kitchen, frolicked naked and noisily in the swimming pool.

She hadn't worried or held back.

All this was to become hers.

But neighbours in South Africa are cautious and observant. It has become an integral way of life. Changes to routines, strangers in the area, unknown cars visiting; all are noted in case the information is required for police reports and action in the future.

The neighbour had seen her arrive and leave - two days later. Had heard the splashing in the pool. And the music. And more.

On the Monday afternoon she quietly told Van Heerden's wife of her suspicions.

'So what happened next?'

Detective Inspector du Plessis shook his head slightly. 'You don't really want to know.'

'Tell me anyway.'

'That same evening Van Heerden phoned Jolene. Told her that everything was over. Dismissed her at the same time.'

'And?'

'Two days later she went to Van Heerden's surgery. It was early and nobody was around. She still had a key. Knew the access code.' The big policeman paused. 'She must have been waiting behind the door when he arrived.'

I indicated that he should continue.

'She...she stabbed him with a butcher's knife. After that she left a message on the answerphone for incoming callers, saying that he was indisposed and would not be in. Then she locked up and left.'

'Did the man survive?'

'Dr Mathee, she stabbed him six times and...and,' he searched for the word. 'And...mutilated him.'

'In what way?'

'She sliced off his genitals. We think he may still have been alive when she did this.'

'My God!' A scene flashed through my dismay. 'There must have been blood everywhere. Surely somebody must have seen her leave. She must...must been covered in it!'

The policeman shook his head. 'No. She wore a boiler suit and balaclava. Even had gloves on and those over-shoes. You know, like theatre staff in a hospital wear.'

'You know this?' I asked doubtfully.

'She stripped them off and dumped them at the scene. Like I said, locked up and left. Clean.' His eyes were fixed on me. I could see something more in them.

'That's not all, is it?'

He shook his head. 'Less than forty-five minutes later she killed Van Heerden's wife and the two children.'

Sitting next to me, Mary Warren had her hand to her mouth.

Du Plessis went on. 'She waited in the driveway, behind a bush. As the woman was getting into the car, she shot them. Three bullets only. They died instantly.'

'Where did she get the gun from?'

'Dr Mathee, this is the New South Africa,' he said caustically. 'Everyone has a gun. Her father gave it to her when she went to university. For self-protection. He also gave her lessons; they practised a lot. She was…is a crack shot.'

Somehow I wanted the saga to end, but knew that there could only be more.

'What happened next?' I asked shakily.

'As far as we can make out, she then stalked the neighbour.'

'And?'

'Later that day she ran her down in the carpark of the Spar supermarket,' he said.

'Killed her too?'

'The woman died on her way to hospital. There was nothing the paramedics could do.'

'And the police couldn't catch her?'

His answer was straight and candid. 'No, we couldn't. She was too quick. Too efficient. We suspect she changed appearance in some way. We know she changed cars.'

'You couldn't track her down?'

'What we later found out is that early the following morning she drove through the Onseepkans border post into Namibia. The next day she crossed from Namibia into Botswana at Dobe.'

'The names don't mean much to me,' I said.

'She chose the more remote posts. The customs people there hadn't even seen our police bulletins.'

The telephone rang, breaking the tension in the room. Du Plessis answered it and spoke rapidly in Afrikaans before replacing the receiver.

'I can give you five, maybe ten more minutes at the most,' he said. 'We will have to be quick.'

'You said she went to Botswana.'

'Yes. I'll have to be brief. She ditched her car in Maun and became a solo tourist. Caught the bus through to Francistown and into Zimbabwe. Another bus to Victoria Falls. Probably walked across the bridge into Zambia.'

'And then she was gone?'

'Not quite, Dr Mathee.'

'What do you mean?'

'In Zambia she met a visiting tourist, a man from Holland. Spent the next two weeks with him. They were married in Lusaka and had a small reception at one of the luxury lodges in South Luangwa. Then she travelled with him back to Amsterdam.'

Detective Inspector du Plessis looked at his watch. 'A whirlwind romance,' he said sarcastically. 'He was about your age. The age you were when you married her.'

'Was?' I had picked up the inflection in his voice.

'She killed him about a year later. He was having a bath and she dropped an electric heater into it. If that was not enough, she then held his head under the water.'

Mary Warren who had been silent throughout, suddenly spoke. 'Does this never end!'

'No, it doesn't,' his voice was ominously low.

I studied him carefully, and mused aloud, 'I wonder what triggered her behaviour. Something must have happened in her youth.'

'Something did,' he said. 'About five years ago I received a phone call from her father asking me to go and see him. I'd previously interviewed him after the murders in Cape Town.'

'A call from her father? That's strange.'

'Yes, I thought so too,' the policeman said. 'But I made the trip. The man was very ill with pancreatic cancer. In a hospice.'

'And what did he want to tell you?' Mary asked.

'He wanted to tell me about another murder.'

'What?'

'Yes. Jolene van der Walt had a younger sister. The day after her first birthday she was found dead.'

The air in the room seemed to go very cold and dry, as if some evil presence was invading, sucking the warmth out. I shivered. I could see goosebumps on Mary's arms.

'The father told me that his wife had been drinking. She passed out on the bed in their room. The baby girl had been in her arms.'

For a moment no-one said anything.

Then Mary spoke. She sounded scared. 'She fell on it…smothered it?'

The image was frighteningly vivid.

'Yes.'

'That is a terrible story.'

'Yes. And that is what it was,' Du Plessis smiled grimly. 'Just a story.'

'I don't understand,' Mary said.

'I do,' I interrupted. 'Jeannie, Jolene must have done something to the child out of some sort of pathological jealousy.'

The policeman nodded. 'That is what the father wanted to tell me. His brother was the local coroner. He did the autopsy.'

'And?'

'The baby had not been killed by the mother. She had been drugged to death - crushed sleeping pills in her bottled milk. Her mother must have found the poor thing before collapsing.'

'This never came out?' I asked.

'No, the brothers kept it quiet. Called it cot death.'

'Why did they hide the truth?' Mary blurted out.

Du Plessis shrugged his shoulders. 'Reputations, small community, church involvement. They closed ranks. It happens.'

'But they must have known that Jolene did it,' Mary stated.

'Later, yes. Remember, at that time, Jolene was only twelve years old.'

'But her father suspected,' I said.

'Yes. When I last saw him he was absolutely certain. Said he had the proof and would get his brother to send it to me.'

'And did he?'

'No,' he shook his head. 'The man died early the morning after I'd seen him.'

'And did you ask the brother?'

'I did. But he said that he had nothing for me. The proof was never found.'

'But did he also think that Jeannie - Jolene - was the culprit? You must have asked him.'

'Yes, he did,' Du Plessis said.

'And now?' I asked. 'What happens now?'

Du Plessis clenched his fists. 'This case has been with me from the day we found she had crossed into Namibia. All these years we have been trying to find her. It will only end when we do.'

'I think...I think I may have been a little lucky.' My voice sounded sheepish. I somehow felt ashamed. 'I wonder why she came back to South Africa with me.'

'These people usually have an underlying arrogance. A belief that they can always out-think others,' he said. 'She probably thought that our records were not up to date. Or that we had closed her file.' He looked at both of us. 'I never close a file. Even when I have all the answers. Even when I have solved a crime.'

'I am sorry to keep you, Detective Inspector,' I said. 'But why did the border official yesterday become suspicious? She has a British passport.'

He opened the drawer again. 'Open her passport,' he instructed.

I did so. Mary looked over my shoulder.

'She changed her appearance,' Du Plessis said. 'Changed her name. But she didn't change the place of birth or date of birth. An original birth certificate is such an important document these days. She was one of only two babies born in Calvinia on 11 August 1980.'

'And so it flagged on your system.'

'And for once the system worked,' he smiled sourly. 'Or would have, if that poor policewoman had been more careful yesterday.'

'I have to go now. Dr Mathee, I urge you to always be vigilant and careful.' He stood. 'Jolene van der Walt, Jeannie as you know her, is probably the most ruthless and cold-blooded killer I have come across in nearly thirty years of police work.'

He moved to the door. 'She is unpredictable and vicious. Take my advice - move to Canada or Australia or bloody Mongolia, just change your life. And, if you do,' he added, handing me his business card, 'let me know where you are.'

***

Her life is sedate and mundane.

The man she lives with farms deep within the Great Karoo. It is a remote yet beautiful place, hours distant from the nearest village. The adjoining farm is virtually derelict, owned by a German businessman who only visits it once or twice a year to hunt.

She took her time in selecting her new husband. Did it by remote control. She trawled the romance websites, scrutinised newspaper and magazine classifieds.

A few she followed up.

His advertisement in the *Farmer's Weekly* magazine was simple and straightforward. 'Lonely middle-aged farmer in good health seeks companion. No children, no ties, no baggage.'

He is a good and self-contained man. Soft-spoken, he handles his new wife, his sheep and his workers with a kind and gentle compassion. They sit outdoors most evenings. Not saying much, their eyes are drawn to the vast coal-black sky with its swathes of coruscating stars.

She will hold his hand to possess him. He asks no questions of her.

She has no past to recall or share.

MISS ITALY

Zanzibar 2016

There is a view down the east coast of Zanzibar where the sea changes colour with the turn of the tides. The scene is one of dazzling pristine beauty. At set times throughout the day it is a vista that expands as the heat of the day builds, then seems to shorten towards dusk when the air starts to cool.

The reef, which is 400 metres offshore and runs parallel to the coast, stretches almost the full length of the island. At low tide the deeper water on the far side is a brilliant azure. Along the beaches on the inner side of the reef the sea colour is a fine lace blue; at times it turns almost translucently white.

***

I had seen her three days in a row now. Always at the same time, always walking in the same direction. There was something about her; she spiked my interest, but quite why I did not know.

I had formed a little routine too. Every afternoon at 3:30pm one of the helpers from the kitchen would bring me a flask of hot water and a few teabags. He would invariably stay and chat for a few minutes. There was always a snippet of local news to share - perhaps the size of fish being caught, a whale shark seen offshore, or an update on the impending general elections.

For an hour or two I would sit there, half-reading half-watching the passers-by on the beach, sipping at the light, fragrant Kenyan tea. The locals often waved and called out; some stopped by and introduced themselves, some I already knew.

Then I would make my way to the little restaurant at Bwejuu where the jovial cook had a meal ready for me.

It was a simple uncomplicated holiday. Running on the beach. Walking between the villages. Going out fishing. Whatever I felt inclined to do.

And it was proving good for me. My mind was easing, the stress I had been through steadily dissipating. All that had happened to me during the past year was fading as I rested and mentally recuperated.

***

The woman's routine also seemed to be the same everyday.

At precisely 3:30pm she would slowly come past, making her way northwards along the water's edge. Always by herself.

I tried to make out her features. She looked darkly attractive in a mature, refined way. Below her long loose-fitting shirt there appeared to be some damage to her right leg; she limped heavily and needed the aid of a walking stick. From what I could see, the thigh and calf muscles looked wasted and slack.

Exactly an hour later she would return, walking slightly higher up the beach as the tide came in, her stick digging deeper into the softer sand.

On the third day we waved to each other for the first time. My curiosity was stirred even more.

All the locals could tell me was that she was on holiday at a hotel further down the beach. 'The hotel owned by the German.' The derogatory inference was clearly pronounced. The man's wife was from mainland Tanzania and he only employed her family members. The Zanzibaris were excluded.

Her leg seemed slightly better as she passed by on day four. She seemed to be a bit more stable. The beach walking was obviously helping the muscle tone and strength. She gave a light-hearted wave and then a small smile. The gesture seemed irresistible; I almost wanted to join her, but my shyness held me back. I just waved back in response.

An hour went by. She did not return at her normal time. I waited a little longer.

Something made me close my book, get a bottle of water and set out after her.

I rounded the first headland. The incoming waves were already lapping the rocks at the foot of the bluff. In less than an hour one would have to find another way back. By then it would be dark. The risk to a lone crippled European woman on an isolated Zanzibar beach was very high - in more ways than one.

My concern growing, I broke into a jog. I began to run a little faster as I made my way around the base of the next cliff.

Her shirt was the first thing I saw. It was wedged under a rock to prevent it from flying away.

I stopped, heard a faint cry and looked around.

She stood on a sandbank about 250 metres offshore. The fast-incoming tide had left her stranded, the sea swirling in eddies and streams as it surged towards land.

I could feel it as I waded in. The current was not particularly strong because the reef held it back, but the depth in the gullies was increasing. I found it quicker to swim through them than to walk.

When I reached her the sea had already started overlapping the bank she was standing on. The increasingly wet, shifting sand gripped at her feet as she staggered towards me. Her face panic-stricken, she grabbed at me.

I steadied her shoulders.

She tried to speak, mouthing a few words. It sounded softly Italian, but I couldn't be sure.

'We will have to swim back,' I said. 'It's getting too deep.'

Tears welled in her eyes. 'I...I no can swim. Make only like this.' Her arms moved in a cramped dog-paddle motion. 'My leg no working properly.'

'That's okay,' I said. 'We'll go backwards. On your back. Hold your stick in your left hand. Move your right arm in a flat slow stroke. Like this.' I showed her what to do - lifesaving training done years ago still remembered.

'I so scared.'

'Don't worry, I'll be behind you. Holding your head and shoulders up.'

'You won't let me go?' she whimpered softly. 'Please don't let go.'

Slowly we made our way to the beach. The push of the incoming tide helped. There was hardly any backwash or pull; it probably took less than ten minutes to float her almost all the way to the beach. Despite the warm sea water I could feel her shivering from anxiety and fear.

As the water became shallower I felt the sand firm under my feet. I stood and lifted her up, carrying her the last thirty metres to where her clothes lay.

She looked gravely at me as I set her down. Her swimming costume had come askew. She straightened it carefully, then raised her shirt to her face and wiped away the seawater and tears.

'The second time in two months,' she said enigmatically.

'We need to get back,' I said, choosing not to ask anymore. 'It's almost dark. And we'll have to walk through the scrub.'

'No along sea?' she queried shakily.

'No. We won't be able to get around the headlands now.'

'You know the way?'

'There is a path up to the village. Through there,' I pointed. 'But it's not smooth, we'll have to go slowly.'

'Sn…snakes?'

I shook my head. 'No, not here. Take my arm.'

We found our way through the undergrowth, the path barely discernible in the gathering darkness. It was hard underfoot. Neither of us wore shoes and the crushed broken shells were sharp and painful. Every so often I could feel her wince as she stood on a sharp piece. Out of the darkness came a strange snuffling noise. I pressed on. There had been reports of feral boars in the area; the last thing we needed was to blunder into one of them.

The woman said nothing, just gripped my arm more tightly.

'I will need to rest,' she panted. 'My leg…'

'Can you keep going a little further?' I asked. 'We are almost there.' I could smell the first cooking fires.

The villagers were startled to see us stumbling out of the dark. Two of the men came forward. One of them recognised me; I had been out fishing with him on his dhow. His eyes were glazed and dilated. Fortunately the *ganja* they had been smoking had not yet made them totally insensate.

'I need some transport, please,' I said. 'This lady has had a problem. In the sea. I need to get her back to her hotel. Do you have a phone? Maybe we can call for a bush taxi?'

He gazed at me, his look a little off-centre. His concentration appeared a little off-centre too. There was a long pause before he replied.

'No phone. Can you ride bicycle?' he asked seriously.

'Yes,' I replied.

'Come.' He led me to a palm-leaf covered shelter. 'You take. I fetch tomorrow,' he said.

Proudly he wheeled an old, battered thick-tyred bicycle into the firelight. It had an extended rear carrier with a piece of boarding fixed to it. No gears or brakes to speak of, but at least the tyres were pumped and firm.

The stoned fisherman pointed solemnly. 'This is a bicycle for five persons. My first son sits here.' He touched the handle bars. 'My second son sits here,' he pointed to the cross bar. 'I sit on seat. And my wife,' he touched the board on the carrier, 'she sits here with baby on her back.'

Then he laughed hilariously. 'Heh, heh. Five persons…heh, heh…This is a people carrier…heh, heh!'

I looked at the woman and grinned. 'Are you ready for this?'

Her lips stared to quiver. I could see the words being formed. *Are you serious?* Just in Italian and not in English. The quivering increased and then she was giggling helplessly, words spluttering as her anxiety and worry disintegrated.

The dynamo light shone a dull yellow as we precariously cycled back to her hotel. We had a few wobbles along the way which I managed to correct without us falling off. She had her right arm wrapped around my waist, and held on to the carrier with her left hand.

Half an hour later I left her in the hotel foyer. 'Will you…' I asked, hesitant and uncertain, 'will you have a drink with me…to celebrate our safe return?'

She studied my face, taking her time before responding. 'I will see you again, but tomorrow. When I more in control.'

She hugged me spontaneously, then turned and limped off.

***

Early the following morning I went and sat outside. The sand was pleasantly warm and soothing between my toes. I leaned back, shoulders pressed against a log buried in the sand and watched as the sky slowly turned lighter. The rising sun cast rubescent hues across the horizon. Slowly the colours changed to pink, then gold, and then the sky became blue and undiluted.

My mind drifted along with the colours: peaceful, to quiet, through to totally at ease.

The fishermen were already out. Three of the local women walked by; they waved and greeted me.

I felt I could live there forever.

***

She was on the beach a little earlier than normal and this time did not walk past. She made her way up the path to my veranda and stood there, a shy almost nervous enquiry on her face.

'Please,' she asked, 'please will you walk? With me?'

Together we sauntered along the beach. We started cautiously, then began to share those special moments that occasionally happen in one's time. A moment of introduction. A moment of exploration. A moment of discovery. A moment of new joy.

One of those few times in life where everything appears to stall, then comes to a standstill. Every tiny detail becomes remembered and important. Every word innocent yet meaningful. One of those times when one can start on a clean page, fresh and honest and correct. Where the baggage of years past can be shed.

We spoke of the inconsequential things - our lodgings, the food, the villagers, how we had slept the night before.

'I wake up in night smiling,' she said. 'When I think of us on old bicycle.' Her voice was deep and melodious, her English diction irresistible and enchanting.

Aryanna was from Italy.

'It's a beautiful name,' I said quietly.

Her face coloured slightly. She made as if to touch me.

When I asked what her name meant, she said, 'Holy One.' And then added, 'But now my faith is gone.'

There would be times ahead, I thought, to ask her more.

She appeared to be tightly wound, emotionally raw, with something more suppressed. Sadness or grief, or perhaps both, concealed.

But she was also an attractive, mature woman, tawny complexioned and compact. Her face was Romanesque with large, widespread, light green eyes. In the sunlight they glowed like burnished emeralds with inlaid darker tinges of verdancy.

Her figure was well-proportioned and taut. The memory of her bare breast from the evening before when her costume had slipped loose bore testimony to that.

On closer inspection, the damage to her leg appeared to be recent. When we sat and rested I could see stitch and puncture marks. The skin and surrounding tissue was newly scarred and still healing.

Although our friendship had only just begun, I had the sense that she felt secure with me, that my presence made her comfortable. She seemed to lean into me as we spoke. Maybe it was because of the fright she'd had the evening before. Perhaps my role in her rescue now gave her the confidence that she could trust me.

Propped on our elbows we watched the mesmerising action of the sea. Sitting close to her, my thoughts and instincts were becoming stimulated and aroused.

The last year for me had been monastic and introspective. I found Aryanna intriguing and beguiling. Was there a kindling of emotional spark flaring between us?

***

The tide was coming in, the waves surging a little heavier through a gap in the reef.

I thought I saw something dark in the water. Just a fleeting shape. Then there were more.

'Watch,' I said to Aryanna. 'Can you see the fins?' I pointed.

She shielded her eyes from the glare. 'Where?'

'Look to your left a little, maybe two hundred metres out.'

Her head shifted and then she spotted them.

'What are they?' she asked excitedly.

'Dolphins. Bottlenose dolphins. Looks like there are about eight or ten of them.'

'Dolphins! First time I see! Ever only on TV!'

'Come.' I stood and held my hand down to her. 'Let's see if we can get closer to them.'

'I…I a little afraid.' But she took my hand and I helped her up.

Taking her walking stick and still holding on to me, she let me lead her into the lapping waves. When the water reached the top of our waists we stopped.

'Let's stand here and see what happens,' I said.

We could see the dolphins clearly now. They were swooping and frolicking, now less than a hundred metres away. To me they seemed to be getting gradually closer. Maybe they were chasing a school of small fish or maybe they had sensed us standing in the water. It seemed that their curiosity also drew them nearer.

In a wide arc through the clear water the leader swung towards us. Two of the others followed. The remainder stayed further out.

Aryanna gripped my hand even more firmly.

Effortlessly the three dolphins swam past us, almost within touching distance. They circled a little closer, their large, sleek bodies glistening muscularly in the afternoon sunlight. Then they circled slowly again.

'Talk to them,' I said softly. 'Say something. Let's see how they respond.'

Aryanna tried to speak but could not. She was totally overcome. Tears streamed down her cheeks, chest heaving as she wept.

I said nothing. I sensed that her distress was rooted in something far deeper. This was clearly not the time for words to be uttered without insight.

We stood there for a few more minutes, watching as the dolphins steadily glided away.

Back on shore Aryanna allowed me to hold her lightly as she slowly composed herself. Like a little girl she wiped her eyes with the back of her fists.

'I have never seen something so beautiful, so wild…so free,' she whispered shakily. 'The wonder. I will never forget. Never.'

Behind us the sun was sinking below the tree line. In twenty minutes or so it would be dark.

'I must get back,' she said. 'Tonight we have tour group dinner.'

My thoughts swirled. 'Is this your last night here?'

She nodded. Holding hands, we walked on for a few more minutes. I wanted to say something, persuade her to stay a little longer, but my throat felt constricted. My natural reserve held me back. I sensed that Aryanna knew it too.

She raised my hand to her lips, gently kissed it.

And then she was gone.

**

I slept fitfully that night. Tossing and turning, awake more than asleep.

When I did sleep there was one dream that seemed to repeat. The memory of it was still vivid when I woke at dawn. In the scene I had just a glimpse of Aryanna's face as she boarded a train - a train that was out of reach and departing from the platform across from where I stood.

I could stay in bed no longer. I made coffee and went outside to think.

The breeze that came off the sea was tepid, but at least it kept the mosquitoes at bay. Out on the dark sea there were small white lights - torches. I could hear the fishermen talking as they made their way to deeper water. Their ancient wooden dhows creaked over the low swells.

My head felt heavy, headachy; it was thumping softly as if I was suffering from a hangover. The only thoughts I had were of Aryanna. Here I was, a man of nearly fifty, acting like a teenager. Albeit, in today's connected world, a very shy teenager.

Most of the night I had been trying to work out if I should go and visit her at the hotel. Or find a way of staying in contact. Little schemes of trying to see her again. But, for all I knew, her group might have left already. I should have made an attempt to find out more about her situation. It just had not been opportune.

With a sigh I stood and went back to my hut. I shook out my running shoes and put them on, then clipped the pedometer to my waistband.

I would run along the road to the next village and from there back up the beach. The exercise would do me good. Fifteen kilometres to clear my head.

**

She was waiting for me when I got back. A note in her hand fluttered to the sand. I bent down and picked it up.

'I so glad you are back,' she said. 'Better than goodbye note.'

'Aryanna…please!'

She stopped me. Placed her hand on my shoulder, then higher, carefully wiping the perspiration from my forehead. A baby's feather-light tenderness in her touch.

'I know what you want to say.' She drew a deep breath before continuing. 'For me is same too.'

'You mean…you mean you would like to…'

'Yes.' Her eyes were iridescent in the sunlight. 'Yes, I would like to stay on. Near you. With you.'

For a moment it seemed as if my heart stopped. As if it had been stilled by excitement and apprehension.

'But,' she went on, 'but I cannot. Is not possible.'

'Why not?' I asked softly.

Her fingers dug into my shoulder. I could see she was close to tears again.

'Steven, in August this year I lose everything. Everything gone.'

'I'm not sure I understand.'

'It is long to explain. The minibus leaves in twenty minutes. To take us to ferry. Then to mainland.'

Her eyes held me. The depth of her sadness and pain were clearly evident.

'Steven, I have nothing. No any clothes. No any money. No any jewellery. No home. No friends. Almost no family.' Her head dropped, the words faint and desperate. 'Nothing anymore.'

I tried to interrupt, but she continued talking, her words staccato through her despair. 'I…I…only have one thing left. Only…ticket back to Italy. Ticket I bought long ago. Ticket…on tonight's plane from Dar es Salaam.'

She took both my hands in her own, unsteady as her walking stick fell.

'Steven, now I go. I have to go. There is no choice.'

I moved to put my arms around her, but she pulled away slightly, then kissed me gently on the lips.

'Aryanna, there are more choices. You can stay here with me. In the next hut. Or...' My words sounded desperate. 'Or I'll come with you. I have money. More than enough.'

She shook her head. 'I go now. These few times with you...' She couldn't finish the sentence. 'But, my pride too. That is all I have left of me.'

She kissed me again. Hard. Twice.

I handed her the stick. She waved once sadly as she made her way back to her hotel.

I felt desolate. Dazed and shattered. I had lost my wife to the past, now it seemed that I had lost my hope for the future.

**

I gathered my thoughts, pondering what to do next.

I knew then that I would have to make a move, take some action. I couldn't wallow in remembrance of what might have been.

Local knowledge was now clearly needed. The cook would help.

We sat at a table in his little restaurant. For a few minutes he listened intently as I spoke. The planning, the conspiracy, was sure to be the hot topic in the village for the next few days.

'Mister,' he said, 'the flights overseas normally leave late at night or very early in the morning. So,' he went on seriously, 'this is what we will do.'

He was clearly enjoying the situation. And his involvement.

'You go pack. Leave money for accommodation with me. I will pay owner later. I arrange taxi for...' he peered at his watch. 'Thirty minutes time. Then taxi take you to Precision Air for two o'clock. If that flight is full you take next one at five o'clock.'

He smiled. 'Either way, this will still be quicker than those who go by ferry. And then those people still have to get from ferry port to airport. Sometimes this can take very long. Traffic in Dar very bad.'

His planning hadn't ended yet. 'I will phone my friend Simon in Dar. He can meet you. Take you to main airport. I tell him to stay with you until you find Miss Italy.'

He paused. 'When that sorted out he will be there to help more if you need him.'

He shook my hand. 'Maybe, God willing, you will both be back here tomorrow.'

***

My luck held.

The cook's suggestions and arrangements had worked like clockwork.

Africa always surprises one.

Simon found a white plastic chair for me. I sat just inside the main door to the departures hall and waited. He went off, returning ten minutes later with coffee in containers and two bottles of water.

'Mister Steve,' he said. 'Nobody has checked through yet. It is still very early. I will stay outside and watch. Maybe I will recognise the group. I will also ask around.'

The late afternoon into evening drew out interminably. I watched the clock. Tried to read, then tried to snooze. And I kept on looking up to watch the clock. I stretched and walked around.

A policeman came over to me and we chatted for a while. He asked me what I was doing there. I explained the situation and told him that I was waiting for someone.

'No problem,' he smiled. 'Waiting is our national sport.' He wandered off, talking and joking with his colleagues and with some of the other people hanging about.

Two hours passed. And then another two. Outside it had gone dark. Almost without my noticing.

Then someone switched on the departure noticeboard. It blinked red and flashed a few times. The letters and numbers settled. There were three flights out that night. If Aryanna was on the last one my waiting would extend to least another six hours.

My eyes were closing now. The length of the day. The travelling. The tension and doubt, the anticipation were all catching up with me.

Were my hopes too high? Was I chasing shadows? They were my last thoughts before I drifted off to sleep.

***

Somebody touched my shoulder. I sat up, startled.

199

Simon stood there. 'Sorry, Mr Steve, please wake up.'

'That's okay,' I muttered. 'I'm awake.'

'Mr Steve,' excitement was clearly evident across his features, 'two busses have pulled into the carpark. The people here say they are the ones that normally collect the Zanzibar tourists from the ferry. Maybe,' he went on, 'maybe Miss Italy is with them.'

'Let's hope so,' I said. I could feel an increase in my heart rate, a rush of apprehension and agitation.

Stay calm, I told myself. *Just stay calm.* I tried to reconcile my thoughts, hoping that this was not just a wild goose chase. *What the hell am I doing here? What if she just wants to go home? And how do you cope with someone else's sense of pride, of their self-worth and self-respect?*

But then her sad words came back to me. Those hollow sounding desolate words: *Everything gone. Nothing anymore.*

I stood to one side and waited. Watched as porters bustled past followed by the departing tourists. They all seemed to be talking at once, voluble and excitable, as I'd always found the Italians to be. They crowded in through the entrance, all deeply tanned and brightly adorned in traditionally styled bangles, wristbands and necklaces.

The first group came through, the tour leader ushering them vigorously towards Customs Control. The second group passed by in similarly ordered bedlam.

I strained, trying to see her. *Had I missed her in the mêlée? I couldn't have.* I pushed my way outside and looked around.

Aryanna stood there alone. Her back was to me, shoulders shaking. She faced eastwards in the direction of Zanzibar, as if she could somehow see it.

As I moved nearer I could hear her sobbing quietly. She sounded so lost and distraught.

I took a deep breath. 'Aryanna,' I said. 'Please Aryanna. Don't cry anymore.'

I could see her go still. Freeze in position.

'Aryanna…'

She turned, her face a study in disbelief. The light was poor where I stood; she struggled to make me out.

'Steven? Steven … is that you?'

'Yes, Aryanna, it's me.' I moved closer.

'Steven,' her voice remained hesitant. 'I can't believe. What…what are you doing here?'

'Aryanna, I've come to be with you. That is, if you will allow me to.'

She looked at me intently, then spoke slowly, her voice tremulous. 'Steven, since I left you this morning, there has been only one thing on my mind. No, I wrong. Two things. Round and round I turn them.' Her eyes probed deep into mine. 'That is why I stand here crying.'

'And those two things are?'

'My pride. And you.'

'And?' I feared what she might say next. Held my breath. Felt entranced, as if standing in some dream world.

'In minibus. On ferry. Waiting in hotel in Dar es Salaam. Now in bus again. I turn them around.'

'And?'

Aryanna dropped her stick and fell into me. Her arms went around me, her words almost lost in my shirt. 'I know now that you will become more to me than my pride.'

I could feel her intensity. It matched my own.

'Please Steven, please take me back to Zanzibar with you.'

***

So began day one of our new lives. That was just over two years ago.

We often talk about what we had been through before that; there is nothing to hide. There are often little things, out-of-the-blue occurrences that we tell each other of, times and memories from our pasts.

On 24 August 2016 Aryanna lost everything.

All her life had been spent in the small town of Amatrice in central Italy. A single woman and bookkeeper by profession, she also cared for her disabled nephew.

The earthquake that struck at 1.36am on that day destroyed everything - her home, her family and her extended family living in the equally devastated nearby Accumoli. Most of her clients were killed as well.

It took five days for the authorities to extricate her beloved nephew's crushed and broken body from the wreckage.

On the night when the earthquake hit, Aryanna had been unable to sleep. A mysterious unease kept her awake. As it struck she was sitting in her small garden with a glass of lime juice. A collapsing wall knocked her down; her right leg was broken in three places.

She was one of the first people to be rescued. Her survival had been fortunate and miraculous.

Eventually she was released from hospital with her leg slowly mending. All she had left was a pre-paid holiday to Zanzibar and a meagre annuity in a cash-strapped Italian bank. The annuity was not due for payout until she turned sixty, and she could no longer afford to pay her contributions.

Aryanna had lived a simple and happy life, devoted to her nephew, but with her family and friends all near. She kept her clients' books up to date and they paid her when they could. Sometimes the butcher gave her meat instead of money. The pharmacist would often dispense the medicine she required for her nephew without asking for payment.

It was a way of life she had enjoyed since leaving college.

Her office had been in her home. Her cash and small personal valuables were locked in a desk drawer.

The earthquake had ended it all.

Somehow my own tribulations seemed less, shocking though they were.

My ex-wife was a serial killer, vicious and dangerous. Alive, missing, the police authorities still unable to find her. National and international warrants were out for her arrest. I had struggled to get my marriage annulled.

Aryanna and I sit outside most evenings. It's always warm. With the sound of the sea in our senses we hold hands and talk, reminiscing, or sharing our thoughts and views on the present and future. Sometimes one or more of our Zanzbari neighbours would call in. *To test your Swahili,* they say. They enjoy Aryanna's amaretto coffee.

And now, both steadily healing, our joy in each other grows unbounded and free. Destiny joined our lives.

Printed in Great Britain
by Amazon